STRAIGHT UPHILL

A Tale of Love and Chocolate

Straight Uphill: A Tale of Love and Chocolate by Jess Wells

Copyright © 2020 Jess Wells

This is a work of historical fiction. While based upon historical events, any similarity to any person, circumstance or event is purely coincidental and related to the efforts of the author to portray the characters in historically accurate representations.

Cover design by Christine Horner

Interior design by Jacqueline Cook

ISBN: 978-1-61179-394-9 (Paperback)
ISBN: 978-1-61179-395-6 (e-book)

10 9 8 7 6 5 4 3 2 1

BISAC Subject Headings:
FIC019000 FICTION / Literary
FIC027000 FICTION / Romance / General
FIC027050 FICTION / Romance / Historical / General
FIC044000 FICTION / Women

Address all correspondence to:
Fireship Press, LLC
P.O. Box 68412
Tucson, AZ 85737

Visit our website at:
www.fireshippress.com

Praise for *Straight Uphill*

"…Wells captures love and longing, death and grief, hope and fortitude in writing that is lucid, clear and immediate. I am in awe of how much is going on in this short novel, and how vividly it is presented."

—**Seymour Hamilton**, author of *The Astreya Trilogy*

"The arrival of a grief-stricken American sparks a series of unlikely alliances in a remote Italian village known only for its chocolates. Sweetly sensuous, the story spins across centuries as only Jess Wells can do, weaving historic fiction into a contemporary tapestry of tale of loss, love, second-chances and chocolate."

—**Nisa Donnelly**, author of *The Bar Stories*

"Author Jess Wells has written an insightful, delicious novel in *Straight Uphill: A Tale of Love and Chocolate*. The reader is engaged in the story from the first page to the last, while contemplating the sumptuous chocolates, delicious Italian meals, and budding love relationships. Along the way, there are some surprising twists and turns. A simply delightful book!"

—**Deborah Lloyd** for Readers' Favorite

"Jess Wells pens a story of love and loss in *Straight Uphill: A Tale of Love and Chocolate*. The narrative taps into one's senses with its Italian scenery and cuisine, especially the decadence of chocolate. It penetrates the heart with triumph and tragedy and tests the soul with history…The stories of love in the quaint Italian village peak and descend, proving love and life are a struggle, and the best way to conquer them is to head "Straight Uphill.""

—**Cheryl E. Rodriguez** for Readers' Favorite

"*Straight Uphill: A Tale of Love and Chocolate* combines two human passions and the compelling allure of chocolate to develop a plot that spans several generations… the plot evolves in the present and melts, like chocolate, into the past…"

—**Emily-Jane Hills Orford** for Readers' Favorite

"*Straight Uphill* is lush, lovely and enchanting, merging past and present with the tang and sweetness of chocolate, and proving that redemption and healing, and even love are there waiting where one least expects it. I had a marvelous time getting wrapped up in this spellbinding and beautifully written novel. *Straight Uphill: A Tale of Love and Chocolate* is most highly recommended."

—**Jack Magnus** for Readers' Favorite

Other titles by Jess Wells

Fiction:

The Disappearing Andersons of Loon Lake

A Slender Tether

The Mandrake Broom

The Price of Passion

Aftershocks

Two Willow Chairs

The Dress, The Cry and a Shirt with No Seams

The Sharda Stories

Run

Non-fiction:

A Herstory of Prostitution in Western Europe

For Steve, beloved

STRAIGHT UPHILL
A Tale of Love and Chocolate

Jess Wells

Cortero
An Imprint of FIRESHIP PRESS

1

It was fitting that the little village required a trudge straight uphill, as Gretchen was weighed down, in the case of her life with tragedy, and in the case of today's sojourn, with a wheeled suitcase so large that she had to wrestle with it as if it were a dogcart. Its size made it clear that, though she thought she was coming for a week, parts of her brain had other plans.

She had chosen this Italian village from a pile of yellowed clippings from the travel section of the *Times* that had lived on her bedside table for more than a year, and while it was a significant decision, she gave it nearly no thought amid the funeral arrangements, flowers, charities, and the visits from well-meaning friends whose horrified looks just reminded her of her nightmarish position. Her son had been killed on a kindergarten field trip, the only one in the school bus who had died, and the singularity of it still perplexed her. She knew that his seat had been the point of impact with the car; she knew the physics of it but still couldn't make sense of it.

After making her the center of what felt like ghoulish attention, the other mothers from the school avoided her, clustered together away from her at the mall with the excuse of a PTA planning meeting that, of course, they said, she would not be attending. Now there was no glass of wine at the kitchen table while children had a play date, no chatting at soccer games. She thought the increasing gulf was sensible, since to witness her grief would be to visit the prospect of their own. Besides, they had traumatized children who, after making paper flowers and singing in a special assembly for their classmate, needed to put the event behind them and resume what their parents called normal life. And the gulf was partly about Gretchen herself. At 35, she was still toned and slender and her long hair was a delicious chestnut color, shining and beautiful, though she usually pinned it haphazardly to the top of her head. Her grief had pulled some of the rosy glow from her face and had dulled the sparkle in her eyes a bit, but the grief made her look like a handsome Irish setter who had been kicked and the fathers at the school were even more drawn to her than usual, wanting to shield her, to pick up the pieces for her. Since her vulnerability was alluring, it was suspect.

For 64 days Gretchen had clutched a bottle of anxiety medication in the front pocket of whatever she was wearing. Her husband Bob had dressed for work every day but sat in his car in the garage staring into middle space, until his sporting goods store was in financial trouble. Bob sold it to his brother who had a bit of money but no interest in it, moved downstate, and sent divorce papers through the mail.

Everyone said she should try harder, fight back against the gray fog of grief that made her feel that she was stumbling, even when surefooted. She had resolved to make progress. She could make it to the next chair. She could make it to the bus stop. She could drive to the grocery store and, after sitting in the parking lot to gather herself, dash in, grab an item (frequently something she didn't need but that was close to the door), and hurry back out. Even months after the funeral, she couldn't shop without resting her forehead on the handgrip of the cart, unable to decide what to eat without her family. Assailed by the bright packaging of food for happy days, she wondered if anyone actually lived that way, as a frightening clown makes you wonder about clowns in general.

Gretchen was an accountant in a small town on the edge of Loon Lake in northern Michigan. The retirees, farmers, and owners of small businesses would come into her pine-paneled office with their handwritten ledgers or envelopes of receipts and she would help them do what was necessary. Never more, never less, and she had always appreciated the neat columns of it, the way her work could be set aside at family time, nothing to ponder after hours since numbers that add up disappear into correctness. After her son Nate's death, though, numbers proved their inability to represent, let alone control, life's chaos. Even linearity had deserted her.

But she had made it to Italy, all the way to this village, in a daze through the airline check-in, through the flight (though to be strapped in was reassuring), through customs and the assault of Italian shouted at her from taxi drivers, through the miles of deep, green scrub tenaciously holding to copper-bright orange soil, and her eventual deposit at the base of this hill.

If she made it to the top there would be a hotel room. There would be a bed to hide in, a door to lock. Halfway to the top of the hill, she plopped down on a stone bench that made the suitcase teeter wildly and tip over onto her ankle. Both her therapist and her doctor had advised that when she became overwhelmed she should simply sit down and rest. Grief takes energy, they said. But she worried that the sudden collapses made her look unhinged: abandoning her spot in line at the bank, dropping blouses onto the floor at the mall to sit in the food court. She spent her time in places where sitting was expected: parks, the library, museums, paying the entrance fee just for the ruse of normalcy in sitting without moving." Still, she suspected that she looked odd (as she was even more oblivious to her good looks than usual) so she took extra showers, dry-cleaned her clothes frequently, overdressed so that she didn't look like a bag lady. Prosperity, cleanliness, and the look of contemplation were the only tricks she thought she had left.

Gretchen sat on a bench in front of an altar to the Virgin Mary that had been cut into a high stone wall, the fluted arch above the statue's head patinaed with candle-black, the hem of Mary's cloak smoothed from the touch of petitioners and supplicants. Gretchen offered no prayers: though there was a little comfort in looking at a statue of a mother who had lost a precious son, nothing would bring Nate back, and she was convinced there would be no relief from her own sadness. The altar was flanked by pots of flowers—some hearty with substantive trunks and rugged red flowers, and some delicate, their petals almost translucent, held up with makeshift struts. There were a few dried flowers at Mary's feet, and pistachio shells on the ground as if someone had been feeding their fear while they prayed. The flowers were tended, but the real testimony of devotion was the altar's position: to come straight down and then struggle straight up again was the real offering, Gretchen thought. The ascent ahead was so steep that the cobblestones were laid in a switchback pattern, a walkway defined by short, stone walls worn by dirt and rain and the expectant shuffle of people through the years. *Since all movement is driven by optimism*, she thought. Probably why she sat still so frequently.

Looking up at the village, though, a tiny smile tugged at Gretchen's lips. The houses were painted aquamarine, a bright golden-yellow, an assertive pink, almost cheerful, brightening her involuntarily as if looking at the silly colors of a merry-go-round. The village looked like a hat someone had crocheted on the top of the hill, a small clustering of buildings that gave way on all sides to steep descents, surrounded by hills with terraced fields. She had picked the village because it was remote, and as she scanned the skyline the village contained the only buildings for miles. A small puddle of people, a tiny pond of a village, densely packed and abruptly ending. It seemed contained enough for her first entrée back into society.

***

Luca, the driver sent by the hotel to pick Gretchen up at the airport, had driven by her several times, mistaking her for one of the crazy people who sat outside the arrivals door as if their peace of mind was about to be delivered. She might be one of the homeless who sloped around the baggage claim as if it was comforting to be around other people who were only a fraction of themselves, who had left the major part of their life behind them. She wore a long, navy blue coat (too warm for the weather) with the collar turned up as if it was her turtle shell. Luca circled the airport again and finally, despite all his internal protest that this slump-shouldered woman staring at the ground could not be an American tourist, he pulled up. Seeing the look in her big eyes, framed by her beautiful hair, his ire at the confusion and wasted time drained away and was replaced by pity, then a softer, more respectful protectiveness.

Luca, a short, squat man in early middle age, had been handsome in his youth, with thick, wavy hair. He'd had a large, bushy mustache since the first day he could grow one, and wore heavy coats with broad shoulders whenever the weather permitted. He spoke up loudly and gestured broadly to take up what he considered his fair share of space. But despite his good looks, being short worked against him, and he now looked attractive but well-worn, like good, broken-in shoes. But, as most women towered over him, he was not the sort that women leaned against or imagined themselves encircled by, which made him more assertive in his protection, a blustering, demonstrative, almost bossy tendency that over the years had sometimes taken on an angry quality.

Today, when he had pulled up beside Gretchen in his old, lovingly-tended Mercedes, he braked softly, closed his door quietly, and stepped toward her as if fearing he would spook a forest animal. She held up a piece of paper to him and he nodded, struggled in his jacket to produce the matching paperwork, and then gently helped her into the backseat, careful to scoop the hem of her coat inside and close the trunk softly. Usually his passengers were chatty tourists and, especially if they were Americans like Gretchen, self-deprecating and curious for his advice, but with this morose and seemingly fragile woman, he kept quiet and drove carefully.

Luca had dropped her off to walk up the back way to the village, having learned over the years that tourists like the long walk up the hill to the hotel. Gave them a chance to appreciate the town. Made it seem more off the beaten path. He probably should've taken her the front way, he thought. Couldn't take her to the hotel but as far as the restaurant three doors down.

If he had brought her that way she would have seen a sturdy though unremarkable church; a shop for cigarettes, milk, postcards and sweets; a struggling bistro that tried to make fish and chips and hot dogs for the busloads of tourists who infrequently arrived; and a single line of homes and apartment buildings, not more than six in total, that climbed steadily upward to the crest of the hill and the rest of the village. The six homes were flanked by a road that was the only one wide enough for delivery vans. It was made of cement (not cobblestone), and in the rain, it acted like a huge gutter, so often channeling water into the church that many wore boots to mass every Sunday. But the real center of the town was the plaza at the crest of the hill with the post office/tobacconist and the hotel, plus the town's pride and joy—the restaurant Giordano Trattoria, and two streets over, Liguria Panetteria. Rain that sluiced off the cobblestones on the other side of the plaza watered the verdant gardens of the greengrocer, who pressed into service every inch of loam with herbs growing in waist-high, stone planting beds and small pots, flanked by spindly fruit trees and yellow-topped vegetables. The greengrocer, from her tiny stone building with a bright red door, slightly downhill from the crest, spent her day tromping up and down the hillside watering and tending, frequently with a woman at her elbow who felt protected and cut off from the village enough to share secrets and news, though the edge of the plaza was just yards away.

With Gretchen though, Luca was angry with himself that he had abandoned his passenger, and he aggressively drove up the road that skirted the town to the north and pulled up in the square in front of the church where he usually parked his car. He slammed his door, got a baguette with ham from the bistro next door, and ripped at it with his teeth. When he realized how aggravated he was, he stuffed the food into his coat pocket though it didn't have a wrapper. He drove back to where he had dropped her and spotted her sitting at the altar two switchbacks away. He called the hotel that was her destination and hollered into the phone, gesturing with his short arms, stroking his mustache as he did when he was angry. They should come down and collect her, what was the matter with them? How heartless could they be, he barked into the phone. It took 20 maddening minutes for a young boy to arrive to help her, during which Luca smoked a dark, heavy cigarette, shuffled from foot to foot, brought out his baguette again, and, picking off the lint and the bits of tobacco that now clung to it, alternated between eating and smoking as he watched and worried.

2

The boy, the youngest of the proprietress, scrawny and a bit baffled by his task, grabbed Gretchen's suitcase though it was as tall as he was when the handle was extended. He chattered away in Italian, calling to her and waving her forward, dragging the suitcase up the cobblestones, shrieking as it fell on his shins and hit his foot.

Gretchen followed behind, wordless, trying not to notice the downy hair on the boy's legs, the dirt on him that made her think that she had interrupted his fun. She avoided the sight of children altogether whenever possible and she was chagrined to be such a burden—a new feeling for her. The tragedy had made her feel victimized by the world, but now, with as much intensity as the pain of the injustice done to her, she felt that she was unjustly forcing herself upon the world.

As she and the little boy crested the hill, though, Gretchen experienced the first moment of relief in months that hadn't come from a prescription bottle. Two- and three-story stone buildings, with their happy paint on all sides except the fronts, faced a stone plaza that formed a semi-circle around a fountain. The side of the plaza opposite the buildings was open to the vista, the hill careening downward without a fence or wall of any kind, into a nothingness that raised the hair on Gretchen's arms. The fountain wasn't grand; a sculpted face of a goateed man with a spigot in his mouth dribbled water into a well-worn trough of layered stone with copper rests for buckets. The soft sound of the water was comforting. The wind sweeping up the hill, though today gentle and warm, was a bit menacing. The branches of cypress trees in pots veered sharply toward the buildings, reminding Gretchen of precarious life and powerful nature. Challenges had barreled up the hill and swept through the labyrinthian streets, the stones worn smooth and blackened, the buildings survivors with thick walls, terracotta roofs, doors with lips from the times of mud streets. Hers was not the first tragedy that had arrived here. Other than the sound of her suitcase on the cobblestones, she heard distant hammering, the erratic flapping of the tobacconist's awning, and the clink of plates and cutlery as a young man set up for lunch at the airy restaurant near her hotel. The old village was quiet and solid, having borne witness and survived. She breathed deeply.

At the hotel, the middle-aged proprietress straightened an ill-fitting wig and ushered Gretchen into a sunny yellow room that had an old four-poster bed, a tall wooden dresser, a leather sofa, and a slightly battered coffee table. A wall of glass doors led out onto a deck with six-foot walls and a recirculating fountain that had birds bathing on its edge, most of whom stayed despite Gretchen's arrival. The proprietress avoided Gretchen's eyes, but pressed an old brass key into her hands. "*Vino*," she said, touching her small-faced watch and holding up four fingers. She smiled a bit as you do to cheer someone while you extricate yourself from someone who is not cheery, and then closed the door softly.

Gretchen looked suspiciously at the bed. If she curled up in the covers she might lose the momentum she had gained to get here. But she was tired, so she threw off her coat and shoes, grabbed a quilt folded on top of the tall dresser, and crawled onto the sofa, facing the glass doors. More birds fluttered to the fountain and Gretchen opened the doors slightly to hear them. It was the first time since the accident that she had lain still to enjoy rather than avoid.

She slept fitfully most of the day, as had become her pattern, which threw all her days off and heightened her sense of dissociation. That first night in the village though, she woke up at four in the morning, clearheaded and surprisingly hungry. She stood on a chair to peer over the wall into the plaza.

There was only one light on: the back kitchen of the *trattoria* a few doors down. She put on a light coat as gingerly as if she had a sunburn and quietly left the small hotel. Perhaps they would have a couple of portions left from the day's dining and would package something up for her. When she approached the door though, she startled a young man in a chef's jacket and hat, his eyes ferocious and his face tight, and with just a glance, he lunged for the door and closed it. She was taken aback and quickly walked on.

She didn't mind the hour even though she was hungry. She liked walking late at night, especially down deserted streets where no one could see her fits and starts, the way she pulled her collar up around her face regardless of the weather or suddenly turned to rest against a wall. Tonight, she worked hard to keep going, to resolutely walk to the end of a street, turn up another, and make it all the way to a junction without stopping. Tiny improvements, that's all she could ask of herself. Maybe the birds had cheered her slightly.

But she wasn't alone that night: as she turned up a particularly narrow street that sloped upward, she came up behind an old woman, half her size, her white hair bright in contrast to her black clothing. Her cane on the cobblestones punctuated the stillness. Just as Gretchen was wondering why the old woman was out so late or up so early, a plastic bag of lemons that she was carrying broke open from the bottom and the woman gave a little cry, steadying herself with her hand on the wall as the lemons tumbled down the street.

"Wait there," Gretchen called, intercepting some of the lemons, moving forward to scoop up the others. The old woman exclaimed, and Gretchen smiled a little in commiseration, but when she walked up with her arms filled with lemons, the old woman immediately turned and gestured to a small door in the wall beside a bakery. She disappeared inside it. Gretchen tentatively followed: it was reasonable enough to ask her to carry them the rest of the way, she thought.

Gretchen stepped through the small door. To the left, a hallway led to the shop and an archway straight ahead took them down into a bakery with a wall of half windows, copper pans hanging overhead, big mixers from another time whose paint had chipped off in places, a wall of massive ovens. The old woman stepped behind a double-wide, double-long metal table. She slapped her cane on top of the table and gestured for Gretchen to unload the lemons. The woman barked at the cold ovens as if they were offending her, threw her hands up at the deep mixing bowls that were clean, slapped her hand on the long table and started to cry.

"*Mio figlio è morto per me.*" She ran a gnarled hand across her face. "*Mio figlio è morto.*"

Gretchen retrieved her phone from her pocket and launched a translation app. *Mio figlio è morto.* My son is dead? Gretchen stumbled forward from the feelings she had been swimming in for months. It had followed her to Italy. She gripped the table.

"My son," Gretchen said slowly as it was something she had had to practice, like a description of a rare disease with a complex name, "my son… was recently…killed. In an accident." She made the statement again into the translation app and held the phone out for the woman to hear it in Italian. The woman was stunned, put her hand to her chest, and made the sign of the cross.

"Gretchen Simonson." She extended her hand.

"Signora Bettina Liguria." The old woman displayed dignity despite her tears. She gestured for Gretchen to sit on a stool and she turned to make espresso on the stove.

Gretchen considered running back to her hotel and her bed. The old woman's statement had made her stomach turn over. But she wasn't going to back away from a grieving woman the way the mothers had back home. They sat on stools on either side of the long work table with tiny espresso cups between them. Signora Liguria clutched an embroidered handkerchief and tried to stifle her weeping; Gretchen was speechless. Just as they noticed the dawn lighting the bakery windows, there was an insistent knock at the front of the building that made Signora Liguria shake her head in refusal, sputter, and wipe at her face. "Customers," she said dismissively in Italian, waving them away.

"Shall I...get that?" Gretchen said. "Let me...help." Gretchen could answer the door at least, and she strode down the low-ceilinged hallway between the kitchen and the shop. Liguria Panetteria was small with a long glass case and shelves along the back that held yesterday's loaves of bread with thin golden crusts. She peeked out the window at a middle-aged woman who wore a raincoat over an apron and who shook the doorknob briskly. When Gretchen opened it, the woman barreled in, taken aback for just a heartbeat by the sight of a stranger before motioning to the loaves of bread, barking in Italian, and then, realizing that Gretchen couldn't understand, just holding up her fingers. She slapped money on the counter, took her loaves from Gretchen, and strode back through the door.

Gretchen tried to lock the door behind the woman but was stopped by another woman who slid into the bakery and looked Gretchen over with puzzlement. "*Dove Signora Liguria?*" But before Gretchen could manufacture an explanation and run it through the translation app, the woman asked another question she couldn't understand, pointing at an empty space on the shelves. She then just waved her hands at the bread, held up her fingers, and set down the money. A man in a suit came into the bakery before the previous customer had left and bought a small *cornetti* and a loaf.

Gretchen took a position behind the counter. Lately, she had grown accustomed to doing things that seemed nonsensical, less driven by logic then at any time in her life. This seemed just another task that was too removed from her own life to consider rationally. Besides, if it helped the grieving old woman, so much the better. Gretchen locked the door behind the last of them and surprised herself as she returned to the kitchen with more purpose in her step than she had had in months.

Maybe she could help. Maybe the translation app would make it possible for her to communicate, commiserate. It seemed logical that it would do that: it was designed to pick up her speech and translate it into Italian (or Hebrew or French or one of many other languages) and to hear Italian and then repeat it in English.

Gretchen placed the iPhone between her and Signora Liguria, and it translated with some accuracy. At first, they tentatively used small phrases with pauses. She and the old woman struggled to make the iPhone loud enough for Signora Liguria and it kept delivering odd words that made no sense. Gretchen had to sometimes restate the words with maddening articulation until the letters that appeared matched what she wanted to say.

"How will I ever manage this?" Signora Liguria lamented, and Gretchen knew she wasn't referring to the phone. Even Gretchen, who knew nothing about bread, knew this frail woman could never produce bread on a commercial scale. Not alone, anyway. And she was less than useless: there was never any telling when the grief would paralyze her.

Signora Liguria paced to the cold ovens, pulled open a door, and stared into the vacant interior as she explained her situation to Gretchen. She had to bake bread. There had to be money coming in. Even a few weeks without income would jeopardize everything. And the village would be without bread. There were no other bakers and none of the shops carried bread because no villager would eat an inferior product when her son's bread was so good. Her family's bread, that is. She knew the recipes and special touches as well as her son. They had been shoulder to shoulder for years until she grew too old and frail. She could do it again, couldn't she? All she needed was someone strong.

"How long are you here?" she asked Gretchen.

Gretchen shrugged her shoulders in indecision. It had been planned as a week-long stay, but she had a changeable ticket and clothing for a month. "I have no plans. I could help you in the shop." Wasn't solidarity the best thing for them both? It seemed a bold move but one that produced another emotion – could it be cheer? A tiny bit of optimism or purpose? "Until you find someone else," she explained.

Shop? Signora Liguria unleashed a torrent of Italian. She needed a baker, a *panettiere*, not a shop girl, a *commessa*.

The two stood over the slim phone on the long table. She had made a mistake, Gretchen said. She had misinterpreted; of course she was not a baker. I'm sorry, *mi dispiace*—the phrase every American learns first, she thought ruefully. Was there another baker nearby who Signora Liguria could hire? What about another relative?

Their tentative discussion, though, was interrupted by heavy banging on the side door where they had entered. Without waiting for permission, a tall man in his 20's strode into the bakery. In his white cook's jacket, Gretchen recognized him as the man who had slammed the door in her face just hours before. Signora Liguria and the young man, Paolo Giordano, shouted at each other. The signora sputtered in anger, scrunching up her face and accusing him as he paced the floor denouncing her in return. Gretchen hurriedly fished in her pants pocket for her earbuds and listened to the translation of the row, reacting three beats behind the conversation and sometimes having a hard time deciphering who was accusing whom. Odd words crept into the conversation and Gretchen had no way of backtracking and correcting the phone's mistakes. But the topic was clear and it stunned her: Signora Liguria's son had run away with someone's wife. This man's wife? Paolo was threatening the financial ruin of the bakery and Signora Liguria was waving her arms and hobbling around the kitchen accusing the wife in question of corrupting her son. She cast aspersions on the woman's virtue at the same time that she boasted about the bakery. Gretchen realized that it wasn't that Signora Liguria's son was dead, it was that to an old Catholic woman in a small town, the sin of adultery meant that her son was dead *to her*.

Paolo put his palms on the long table. His thick black hair hung into his eyes, his rolled-up shirt sleeves revealed strong arms.

"And who is this?" he asked Signora Liguria, gesturing at Gretchen.

Bettina straightened, lifted her chin and said imperiously, "*Il mio apprendista.*"

"Your apprentice," he said mockingly in English, looking at Gretchen with raised eyebrows. "You're a pastry chef? You bake Italian bread? Where did you go to school?"

The Betty Crocker aisle, Gretchen thought, starting to panic. If she helped Signora Liguria with the baking, it would be the ignorant coupled with the frail. But Signora Liguria unleashed a new torrent at him: their bread would be even better, he would see, and she had had far too much of the chef's family meddling with the Liguria family already so rather than demanding answers of her he should go back to his watery minestrone and his chewy lasagna. Bettina shooed him toward the door. Gretchen watched his face soften, grow slightly amused at the hyperbole of the old woman. Just before he closed the door behind him he looked back at Gretchen with a dubious little smirk.

Signora Liguria was newly energized, waving at Gretchen to put the phone back on the table for another translation session. They would do this, she said, they would show him. They would show the entire town. Until her son came back, Gretchen would help out.

"Oh no," Gretchen waved her hands to stop the woman. "A *commessa, non un panettiere.*"

Signora Liguria stomped toward the shop and took a quick inventory, then shook her head, a little deflated. There was very little there, but she stood tall when she returned to the kitchen. "My son is on vacation," she said firmly, and Gretchen realized that even if the entire village knew the truth, which would likely be before sundown today, at least Signora Liguria could pretend that she didn't know, that her son was protecting his mother from the sin, so she could maintain her position as a Catholic in good standing. Signora Liguria ordered Gretchen to put a full kettle on to boil and turn on the ovens.

Bettina Liguria, wringing her arthritic hands, felt her rage dissipate slightly. Her son with a married woman. He was a widower, 60 years old, having lost his wife and baby decades ago. Despite years of pressure from Bettina, he had never dated nor spoken of anyone; it seemed to be a topic that had been dropped so long ago that it was hard to imagine that he could be loved like that. Had he been duped? Had he jumped into this arrangement as his last chance? The sin of it!

And yet, she thought bitterly, settling for poor love seemed to be a family tradition. There hadn't been a marriage made of great love since her grandmother in World War II. Among the family, that marriage was discussed infrequently, told like a fairy tale. The light in the lovers' eyes was described as a freak of nature. Her great-nieces and their mothers recounted it in hushed tones, incredulity mixed with longing. Bettina herself was too young to remember it except as a nameless, shapeless glow, like great riches that are lost when you are a toddler. As she remembered it, her grandmother had been withdrawn and pitiful, some said from love and others said from the war. In either case, Bettina grew up feeling as if love could be dangerous. Her father had died before she knew him, and she had never heard her mother speak of her love for him; her mother never remarried, never lit up when conversing with or about someone, never blushed or flirted. Thinking about it now as she hadn't before, Bettina thought that her mother had slid easily into her position as a widow and had chosen to stay there, as if love was a sport she chose not to play or a food she wouldn't eat. Her own marriage, well, it had produced the greatest of loves— a mother for her child—and she couldn't complain when that was the case. Even today. Maybe especially today with the brokenhearted American here. No matter where she was from, a mother deserves comfort. She must be so lost without her little boy. Surely Bettina could help her by giving her a few tasks.

Customers started knocking at the door in increasing frequency and Signora Liguria reassured them: not to worry, tomorrow's bread will melt in their mouths. Paris, London, a grown man doesn't tell his mother where he's going; the chef's wife on holiday as well? It is summer—half the world is on vacation. Within an hour, she had sold all the remaining stock and locked the door, pulled the shade. Should we put a sign on the door, she asked her new apprentice? "Baker on vacation?"

No, Gretchen advised and pecked at her phone, "*Venduto.*" All things of quality are eventually 'sold out.' Bettina smiled, wrote it with a flourish on the chalkboard in the window, and as she marched back into the bakery, she swapped her customer apron for a heavy, baker's apron that she folded thickly in the middle to make it short enough for her. The water was on a low boil and the ovens were getting hot.

3

Surely there was another baker in the area who needed a job, Gretchen hoped. In the meantime, the request seemed straightforward enough: muscle, Signora Liguria had said. She just needed Gretchen's muscles, probably not for long. And even though it turned out that the Liguria boy was alive, her initial connection with the woman as grieving mothers wasn't something she could easily toss aside. What could it hurt if she helped out a bit?

Signora Liguria gestured at pots, tubs, and spoons. "We begin. We are hours behind."

Signora Liguria did all the measuring, rolled all the loaves, inspected every move. Gretchen did all the heavy lifting, punched down the dough. When Gretchen was suddenly paralyzed by waves of melancholia, Signora Liguria refused to let her sit, told her precisely what to do.

Six hours later, however, Gretchen had burned four loaves, dropped dough for another three down the side of the mixer, scored the tops of two in such a ragged way that they had to be thrown out, and had generally driven Signora Liguria to her wit's end. They were both covered with flour; Gretchen had yeast crusted on the side of her neck. Signora Liguria was massaging her swollen hands as they stood on either side of the long table, regarding the paltry output.

"I'm so sorry it didn't go well," Gretchen said through the app. She was filled with misgivings, but she noted that she had gotten through several hours without the fragility of the previous months. She might feel remorseful for her inability, but she was grateful for the unexpected work.

"Sorry?" Bettina Liguria waved a hand at her new employee. She lifted the loaves and thumped their bottoms to listen for a proper bake. She nodded; not the quantity she needed, but the quality was still there. It would have to do.

Bettina gingerly lowered herself into an overstuffed chair in the corner of the kitchen. "Bring the phone." She waited for the beep and the green microphone of the app. "You think in one day you can learn what my family has been doing for generations?" She waited for the phone to translate, wondering if she was being too harsh. What she did not say out loud was that the day had proven that her anger at Paolo's denunciations had driven her to make the wrong decision—it took more than just muscle.

Bettina softened slightly, thinking of the good deed she was doing, the glow in Gretchen's face that hadn't been there when Gretchen recounted the story of her son's death. "It's a good recipe," she reassured Gretchen. "It has suffered at the hands of incompetence before and will survive this time as well." Hooking her cane on the armrest she slowly took the pins out of her hair, wincing a bit and making prideful denouncements of the family of her son's lover as well as all the people who ate pre-sliced bread and the world that ignored the pain of old women.

She slowed her tirade. The recipe had come over the mountains, she continued, her husband's father's great-grandmother, all the way back to the medieval, itinerant bakers who had wheeled their clay ovens between villages. That was his family legacy: master bakers.

Her white braids fell to her shoulders and she massaged the tender skin of her head. Left alone at this time of life? It was a disgrace and a sadness she hadn't thought she would face. Her husband—base and crude—had died at the foot of the hill, struck by a livestock truck, and either no one knew or just ever revealed why he was there in the middle of the night in his best shirt and his Sunday shoes. And now her son had dishonored the family by surrendering to his baser instincts in defiance of God. Bettina knew that at 78 years old she should just close up shop, live out her days on public assistance, sit with the other widows in a tiny park on the backside of the hill between the greengrocer and the switchback lane. With nowhere to go and nothing to do, it seemed like the women were waiting on a bench for death's bus to pick them up. Bettina took the steeper route on the far side to the greengrocer just to avoid them. No, the bakery had to continue; she needed the money, and, more importantly, she needed the work.

Gretchen wasn't sure what she had gotten herself into, but the energy and the clarity of just the last few hours that she had spent baking were precious, enough to consider repeating. "Is there another baker you can call?"

Bettina straightened her shoulders in defiance and looked away. Gretchen sighed.

"Ovens on at 5 tomorrow morning." Signora Liguria rubbed her face and her eye sockets. "You're coming, aren't you?"

What could it hurt if she returned, Gretchen thought? Maybe she would do a better job the next time, and apparently, Bettina didn't mind that it had been such a disaster. Gretchen nodded and gave Signora Liguria a small smile. She hung up her apron, tried to tidy her hair slightly, and stepped back out onto the street.

For a change, she was tired in a good way. The fatigue was in her muscles rather than her mind. Her back was sore, her arms were tired, but now she had somewhere to go and somewhere to return. And she was hungrier than she'd been in months, and grateful for the way that it propelled her back to the *trattoria* near her hotel. The accusatory young Paolo worked there, she knew, and she hesitated slightly, wondering if there would be more histrionics. But a customer is a customer, right? And with every step the air was more fragrant: butter, garlic, onions, wine, beef. Herbs she couldn't identify. She inhaled deeply and quickened her pace, but as she neared the restaurant, she realized that her flour-covered clothing would not be appropriate among the luncheon diners—the well-dressed business people and dapper older couples at the outdoor tables. Gretchen looked away and hurried into her hotel to change.

She haphazardly ran a cloth over her face and dug into her nearly untouched suitcase for a rayon dress that traveled without wrinkling. She was lightheaded with hunger as she struggled into a pair of heeled sandals and headed back to the restaurant. She climbed onto the first tall chair at the bar, unwilling to take up a full table and still too fragile to be in the middle of a jovial crowd.

"*Solo?*" A young man asked her with more incredulity than she would have gotten in the United States. Luckily, it was not Paolo.

"Yes, yes." She struggled to not think about the rest of her solo life, to hang on to the energizing structure of her day in the bakery. The man behind the bar was asking her what she wanted, she imagined, and, at first, she became flustered, almost castigated herself for not having learned any Italian before arriving, but then she saw the chalkboard and waved at it.

"Ah, *menu del giorno*," he said.

"*Sì*." It looked like a meal, didn't it? Not just a list of entrées to choose from. It would be too crass to hold the phone up to the menu to translate, and she was too weary to type the words in. Whatever he brought she would eat. Her courage was waning, but he smiled at her with more brightness than she expected and insisted she have a glass of wine.

The first course of vinaigrette cucumbers brightened her mouth; the small cup of lobster bisque was buttery and soft on her tongue. When the entrée arrived, she wasn't sure whether she had just been softened by the two previous courses or whether the entrée was, in fact, one of the most sumptuous things she'd ever eaten. After the first bite, she put her hands down and looked at her plate. Surely it was just something simple like any other kind of food—a thin slice of meat in a wine sauce—and yet when she put another bite in her mouth, she felt as if a shawl was being put over her shoulders. The food was kindness. It was solace. She stroked her throat and then, assuming she was making a spectacle of herself as she delighted in the food, she opened her eyes and smiled sheepishly. She studied every forkful as it disappeared from the plate.

"Exquisite. *Squisito*," she said as she got down from her tall chair and laid the money on the counter. But it seemed that any emotion was followed by sorrow, or at the very least, that a grief had exhausted her so deeply that she couldn't maintain any other emotion for long. Any transition from event to event became a space into which grief insinuated itself. She struggled to back out of the restaurant without tearing up and was glad that her hotel was so close. Back in her room she peeled off the dress, kicked off the shoes, and allowed herself for the first time to climb into the bed instead of the couch.

***

Before dawn the next day they dove into their work with as much strength and vigor as they could muster.

The phone app, because it was their lifeline, took a hallowed position in the kitchen. To protect it from moisture and ingredients, they reasoned, it needed to be on a special table; to keep it up at the level of their mouths all the time so they only had to walk over to it and not touch it with anything more than a pinky, they moved it on top of a box and put a cloth napkin underneath it. It looked like it was sitting on an altar. Then, because they understood that the Italian would be shown on one end and the English on the other, the two women started collecting their little personal effects on either side of the table: the hotel keys and a little change purse that Gretchen's husband had bought her when they had visited the Taj Mahal; a lace handkerchief and a little porcelain bird that Signora Liguria kept in her pocket.

At first the translation app barked strict orders from Signora Liguria to Gretchen. "Bring that big sack over here to the mixer!" "Pour in half of that five- gallon jug."

"Write it down please. Write the recipes down."

"And allow them to be stolen? Foolish girl."

Gretchen was amused to be called a girl, at 35, and it heightened her vigor to be around someone so much older that Gretchen appeared to be vigorous. She had lost her accounting business (abandoned her business, really, or relegated it to the reality of a life in which she no longer believed). She hadn't protested when Bob left and she'd signed the divorce papers without reading them. Before her departure, she had been a husk of a woman.

However, soon the phone app was translating these questions: "Isn't there a smaller bag? I can't lift these." "Isn't there some way to bring it over on a trolley? I can't lift this, I can't carry this."

Signora Liguria sat down in her flowered chair. There were a dozen loaves in the oven, and hopefully some of them would pass inspection. The signora had rolled the *cornetti* herself so they should be fine, but Gretchen imagined that the old woman's hands were on fire with pain.

There was a similar flowered chair on the far side of the kitchen, and Gretchen, emboldened by her consternation and what now felt like the presumptive way she had been roped into this endeavor, dragged it next to her mentor. Gretchen wiped her face with the inside of her apron.

"Can we make smaller batches?" Gretchen pleaded.

Signora Liguria folded her hands in her lap with irritation and shook her head angrily. "At that scale, we may as well shut the place. And we can't shut the place."

Gretchen considered Signora Liguria. Maybe she had contractual obligations, rent to pay, business debt that was cruelly left behind by her son. Maybe living without her son was enough of a jolt to the woman, and the loss of the bakery as well would just be too much. Gretchen could certainly understand that. It was none of her concern really, but when she saw the woman totter on her cane across the bakery, Gretchen wanted to jump up and move things out of her way, to sit her down with tea and find a blanket for her legs.

But Gretchen was an accountant, and this was a business. Couldn't numbers solve this problem? "What we need is something that is smaller but more expensive," said Gretchen. Not hard to lift, with more of a profit margin.

Signora Liguria snorted, grabbed her cane, and struggled to her feet. She opened a small drawer in the table between them and retrieved a lace mantilla and a rosary. She gestured toward the back door and, muttering but not bothering to be heard by the translation app, she resolutely started for church.

Gretchen sighed. Maybe there was something delicious at the café next to her hotel. She waved toward the back of Signora Liguria, "I'm going for lunch," but the woman showed no sign of hearing or caring.

Bettina Liguria marched toward the church, her cane stabbing the ground more than supporting her. For 61 years, it had been all about bread, and now that her son Angelo had run off, she felt like she had been dropped off at a crossroads with no signs. She was furious with Angelo (her precious angel), her husband (gone three decades now), and bread (that had financed her entire adult life). But she was frightened by the alternative idea that had leapt into her mind as soon as the American had told her to think of something small and expensive. She was too old to start again, but on the other hand, this was her last chance. Did she have the courage?

4

Gretchen hung her apron on the peg, and when she stepped out of the bakery with her little change purse, she slapped at the flour on her skirt and tried to brush it off her arms. She fluffed up her hair a bit then started straight for the restaurant. Three steps into her journey and the smell of grilled seafood wafted over her. She was relieved to see workers in their overalls, and she craned her neck to see inside the kitchen. Who was working this kind of magic?

She was surprised when Paolo stepped out of the kitchen and, without looking at her, stepped forward toward his new customer. When he saw that it was Gretchen, he was taken aback for a moment.

He reached beneath the counter and pulled up an empty basket. "No bread, apprentice," he said in English. And he slammed the little basket back into its hiding place.

"No, *mi dispiace,*" she said.

"What would you like?"

She couldn't remember the phrase for meal of the day and she had left her iPhone behind, so she just gestured at the place in front of her, hands in the air. "Whatever you think is best."

He gave her another look of irritation, then relented, pulled out a wine glass, poured her a bit from the house bottle, and retreated to the kitchen.

He brought her a very small plate of asparagus with slivered almonds and butter. Then he brought her a plate of grilled anchovies that melted in her mouth. She resolved to have anchovies daily for the rest of her stay. He set down a small bowl of raviolis with evenly scalloped edges of dough and a perfect puff, and when she cut into them with her fork, there was an aromatic rush of soft ricotta cheese and lemon zest. Another meal of the most sensuous food she'd ever eaten.

She leaned her head on her fist and closed her eyes, and when she righted herself, regarding her from inside the kitchen, wearing a chef's jacket and apron on which he wiped his hands, was the chef. Not Paolo at all, but a man her age and so clearly the younger man's father that she had the sensation of having slept while Paolo grew up. Same lush, wavy hair, longer than his son's, gray at the temples, held back by a low chef's hat. Trim with broad shoulders. The chef's eyes were agate green but as startling as his son's blue ones. He seemed to be amused by her, and she was embarrassed to be swooning over his cooking. He smiled. She raised her wineglass. "*Delicioso*, chef," she said with deference and a little smile.

Paolo passed him as he brought her a small bowl of *zabaione* and an espresso. He looked back at his father, whose face suddenly clouded over.

"Who would leave such a man?" The son gestured angrily toward his father. "And for an old baker."

Gretchen was confused. "Your mother?"

Paolo grumbled his anger in Italian than pointedly asked her in English, "How is it that you're…an apprentice to the Liguria family?"

She didn't want to dishonor Signora Liguria, but anyone could tell that she was just a tourist, not a baker. "I helped her out in the middle of the night and now seem to be…embroiled in something." Gretchen knew she would return as long as she was needed. "Which is fine. I don't mind helping."

Paolo looked at her dubiously. His father returned to the archway between the kitchen and the bar where she sat, regarding her once again. She dabbed at her lips with her napkin, fussed in her seat to leave, anything but meet the chef's eyes.

"*Molte grazia*," she said to both men, and she hurried back to the bakery.

***

Signora Liguria had two cups of espresso and the iPhone's altar on the little table between their chairs when Gretchen returned. The American woman looked flustered, distracted, Bettina thought. She gestured to Gretchen to put in her earbuds and listen.

"My people were not bakers. My people," she pointedly straightened her bearing, "were chocolatiers. None of this yeasty, fatty…" She waved her hands dismissively. "That was my husband's side. Years ago, it was a good match: the baker's grandson with the chocolatier's granddaughter. My grandmother Caterina—it was said that she could make shapes from chocolate so thin you could see through them. You know how difficult it is to work with chocolate like that?" Bettina smiled wickedly. "Chocolate is the cruelest food. Temperamental. It will not tolerate even the tiniest drop of water. Temperature just exactly so. When you are a chocolatier you are truly great. But my husband, he came from a different line. They haul sacks like at the boat dock, beating the dough with their fists. Stink of yeast everywhere. It's not refined. Not like chocolate. Chocolate is mysterious."

"In your bakery…did you work in chocolate with your husband?"

She stomped her cane on the floor as if she were scolding her family. "Little slabs he would let me put inside his *cornetti* but nothing more. A smear."

Bettina had no memory of either her mother or grandmother ever baking or working with desserts in any way, so she had been surprised when her mother, Maria, had encouraged her to marry the son of the village baker, even though he was a homely and insecure young man. As a wedding present, her mother had given Bettina a wooden box

37

filled with the family's chocolate molds and tools as if they were sacred relics, and Bettina had always thought that her response to her mother's gift had been inappropriately bland.

When she had mentioned to her husband the idea of her offering chocolates at the bakery though, he would have none of it. There was no room, no time, no need, the arguments went. She was needed at the counter—the pretty face at the cashbox—but when she saw the way the villagers shook her husband's hand as if he were an artist, she knew it was because the bakery gave him a notoriety he would not share. Besides, he liked to point out, she didn't actually know how to be a chocolatier.

Six months into her marriage, when her husband was being particularly boorish and then left on a week-long hunting trip, Bettina got out the wooden box, bought a small quantity of chocolate, and practiced. And failed. She hid the spoiled chocolates by wrapping them in paper and putting them in a neighbor's trash can. Her fondant looked like sand, her chocolate streaked and separated. On the third full day of work, a day so overcast that it seemed that the alley out back and the street in front were filled with clouds, Bettina practiced tempering chocolate again. She was surprised when the chocolate responded. Pouring it carefully into her molds, with a scraper and offset knife, she was happier than she remembered ever being. The next day her caramel was soft and buttery; by the end of the week her cream fillings melted in the mouth.

For months afterward, while her husband napped in the late afternoon in the far bedroom upstairs from the bakery, she rolled up a rug at the base of the door to seal off the aroma and made micro batches. She never showed them to him, never sold them from the shop, but, instead, packed them in small boxes the way she had been told that her great-great-grandmother had, secreted the boxes inside beds of straw in small bags, and carried them in her shopping basket to the greengrocer on the far end of the village. At that time, the greengrocer was a homely woman, Bettina's age, with no husband nor hope of one, a woman whose brother was the only other member of her family to survive the war. Did she know of a way that she could sell her chocolates, Bettina asked her, though not here, not anywhere it would be known?

When the greengrocer responded with just a shrug, Bettina gave her one of the buttercream-filled chocolates, then watched the woman's face soften and grow incredulous: why not in the bakery?

"My husband..." Bettina began but the greengrocer nodded with resignation. There was no sense explaining things tied up with men's permission. The greengrocer bit into another piece and considered. Her brother ran a grocery in the next village and could sell them there, for a cut of course. A deal was struck. For 18 months, Bettina made confections every day, increasing their variety and complexity while the greengrocer begged her to make larger batches. Even when Bettina was heavily pregnant, she walked every day to the greengrocer, returning with an herb or vegetable that could arguably be found nowhere else and would serve as justification.

It had been a surreptitious activity that she had no time for after her son was born, and it was not included in his training as his father's baker. As her marriage deteriorated in quality (though remaining intact, of course, as good Catholic marriages should), the chocolates became the symbol of all things refined, things that were especially hers; while the grunting, foaming, heavy-lifting, and the yeasty stink of baking became more and more onerous.

Sitting with the American, Bettina struggled up and Gretchen took her elbow. "Come, *venire*," Bettina gestured with her cane toward the wall behind their chairs. "Move these. Away, away from the wall."

When Gretchen obliged, Bettina bent close to the wall and grasped a tiny latch that opened a triangular cupboard, revealing four shelves of old copper pots. With a sweep of her cane, Bettina ordered Gretchen to retrieve the contents and carry them all to the large table. It took several trips: Gretchen's knees creaked as she bent to retrieve all sizes of double boilers of dark copper, with insets of heavy ceramic, some with lids, some with pour spouts or ladles.

Behind them on the shelves was a long row—stacked half a dozen high—of chocolate molds in the shapes of roses, hearts, squares, multi-layered circles, each one of them burnished with age and heavier than anyone made anything anymore. "They're beautiful," Gretchen said. She laid them out in a row that mirrored their positions in the cupboard. Bettina waved her back to the wall. Next to emerge were pitchers filled with dozens of thin forks, prongs and circular shapes Gretchen had never seen, tiny brushes (a few that were a bit mangy), offset knives, and scores of spatulas. Wire baskets of little empty lidded jars, tiny glass pitchers. Gretchen returned to the cupboard without being asked.

"Oh, I'm sorry, Signora, the plates have all broken." She gingerly lifted the first stack of long narrow plates, their hand-painted floral edges interrupted by cracks their length and breadth. She held the stack in her hands like a dead sparrow. Bettina muttered her disappointment, and, grabbing a large baking pan, she let one end crash on the floor and dragged it noisily to Gretchen. Stack after stack of plates were carefully transferred to the pan, while Bettina stood behind the table as if to shield herself from the shattered ware.

Bettina's voice lost its anger and righteous indignation when her eye caught the burnished edge of something in the depths of the cupboard. "*Un altro.*" Another. She pointed. Gretchen had been sitting on her haunches while retrieving the other items, but she was unable to reach this new mystery without getting down on the cold floor and putting herself into the cupboard up to her waist. It was a box of dark wood, nearly as long as the cupboard itself, four inches deep, with copper edges, most of which were dark with patina. When Gretchen pulled half of it out, Bettina clasped her hands together and muttered a prayer of gratitude. Extracting the rest and struggling to her feet, Gretchen handed the box to Bettina. When she opened the box to reveal the scores of recipes written in a beautiful hand, smudged with butter and chocolate, yellowed with age, Bettina wrapped her arms around the box and smiled.

5

Adelina Giordano heard of her mother's departure from her brother Paolo, who delivered the news curtly, without embellishment. She'd sputtered, dumbstruck, and when she demanded explanations, her brother announced his ignorance and hung up. Adelina had immediately driven in the rain from Rome to the village. She cried half the way, sideswiping a rubbish can in her neighborhood but not bothering to see if her car had been damaged, and when she hit the freeway, she dug for tissues that, when wet, she threw vehemently to the passenger side floor, though they floated in defiance of her anger.

Her father's inattention must've driven her mother away, she reasoned, and for the rest of the drive she built up a rage. He didn't appreciate their mother; he treated her like a sister, a roommate who was necessary but generally unwelcome, a condition that he could remedy if he wanted.

By the time she exited the freeway and started up the mountain, she had thrashed around in her mind enough to know that she wasn't thinking about her parents, but about her own relationship with her boyfriend Antonio—with whom she had run away when she was 16—and it made her feel as desolate as the increasingly dry and rocky landscape. Like mother like daughter, and so her mother had to have been neglected, hadn't she? As she gripped the wheel and admonished herself to slow down before she veered off the winding road, she thought of her mother finding great love again, living a revitalization of passion and romance, the heady feeling of being blinded by lust, unable to think straight because of the overwhelming memory of cologne, logic derailed when recalling someone's touch.

Where on earth was her mother going? Incredible that she had left no word for her children. But she thought her mother was brave to flee a town full of prying eyes and religious judgment, and it was especially brave for her mother, who had rarely ventured outside of the village, and had never lived anywhere else. She had taken a few vacations but had generally returned happy to be home. Wherever she was, Adelina was excited for her; part of her rushed off with her mother, ebullient, giddy with the struggle of battling both the guilt and the lusciousness of her lust—she understood her mother's feelings and she cheered her mother on as she had cheered her own teenage self. *Fly away! Be someone better in a place more deserving.* For her to follow an even more scandalous path than her daughter (though social mores were more forgiving now than nearly 10 years ago) she must have been driven to it by extreme cruelty. Or drawn to it by an astounding love. Either way, Adelina would champion her mother's cause as it had been her own in the past and, in some small part of her mind, she held hope that a genuine, long-lasting, and overriding love might be hers in the future as well. She was 25, as thin as a model, a little sparrow of a woman, and her wavy dark hair hung to the middle of her back. Men confessed to obsessions over her eyes, her legs.

That was the thing about desire, she thought bitterly: even though you know it's not possible, somehow you believe that the way that early love makes you feel will be the way that you will always feel. In her own case, her escape from the village (because that's how it had felt—like a jailbreak) had been at a time when she was so young that the excitement of clandestine meetings was heightened not just by the uncertainty of new love and the unlikelihood of privacy, but by the fact that she was out beyond her bedtime, on a school night, that she had changed out of her little plaid school uniform into something she had spent too many classroom hours devising and that was far too old for her age. The discovery of her love for Antonio had felt like she had burst out of a box, that she had become a person of her own making, someone individuated from her family and her father. The love grew mixed up with the feeling of freedom and purpose, the belief that this was the first thing she had ever done for herself, by herself, that was entirely about herself.

Her boyfriend had seemed worldly, but she knew now that it was just his car and the suits he insisted on having tailor-made even when they struggled to pay the electric bill. It was vanity, not worldliness.

She pulled into a gas station, and as she got out of the car, all heads turned her way. She fell into a quiet though not peaceful state, aware of their regard like a gazelle sensing lions. The man at the next pump spilled gas on his shoe as he watched her. The attendant rushed out to assist her though that service had been discontinued years ago, and she noted in the corner of her eye the mechanic and his assistant, who appeared from the garage and leaned on the front of the car they were fixing while the mechanic wiped his hands on a dirty rag with a predatory rhythm. She thanked the attendant with a smile that she knew was more valuable than the currency being exchanged, and as she got into her car and pulled away, seeing the immediate release of the men back to their tasks, she accelerated too quickly and shot stones out behind her tires. Allure, seduction, manipulation, lust, objectification—what a pathetic dance. And Adelina was chagrined now by the gluttonous way that she had fed her ego on her boyfriend's compliments, on the feeling of superiority his attention gave her, the validation that he provided through his desire. She stomped on the car floor with her left foot, but it seemed more petulant than cathartic.

When Adelina had run off with Antonio she had never felt more beautiful, but what she hadn't known at the time was that she would never feel that beautiful again. Not at filling stations or street corners, even at parties when men filled their glasses upon seeing her. And, running off all those years ago, she had felt brave, as if she had done something important, fleeing the small town as if running was, by itself, an accomplishment of some import when, in the end, she wound up in just another apartment that needed to be cleaned and mopped, with a garbage disposal, a bed with sheets to wash, bills that came in through the slot of her door in Rome the same way they would've come in through her door in the village. But in the village, she would have known the postman and invited him in for a little Christmas wine, remembered his birthday as he did hers.

And, of course, everyone told her that a man who will run away with one woman will run away with another because it's the running that he loves, but she hadn't believed it. She'd thought she was different, that she and Antonio were soulmates (*oh, how pathetic*). She'd really believed him when he said it would be the last time he would run, and again, her newly-fed ego believed that she had cured him, ultimately satisfied him.

She parked her small car just outside the stone wall of the yard behind the restaurant. Though she walked into the kitchen spoiling for a fight, her father was at the market and Paolo was chopping onions with a pyramid of celery and carrots at his elbow.

"Where is she?" Adelina stood with her hands on her hips, affronted. "I've called her a hundred times. Number no longer in service."

Paolo looked to the ceiling and threw his hands up.

"What the hell happened?" she persisted.

Paolo put the knife down and grabbed his infuriating sister by the elbow, steering her over to the linen station where she had spent most of her youth folding napkins into flower shapes. They both faced forward for a bit of privacy and, instinctively, his sister began folding. He had no idea what happened, he said. When had this whole thing started? And how long it had been going on? The baker was nearly old enough to be their mother's father. How disgusting.

"It's not disgusting. It's love," she said pointedly. "Papa must have neglected her."

"Of course," he said mocking her. "It couldn't be that a spoiled woman has run off and left others to work like dogs, could it?" Old wound, he knew. Damn her. Adelina had left Paolo enslaved to the restaurant. They knew their mother was overly dramatic and impractical, that she could fly off the handle and do outrageous things on a moment's notice: buy furniture they couldn't get in the door, send so many things to charity that they had no winter coats. And his sister was just like her. Paolo had gone over to the bakery in the hopes of finding clues as to where their mother had gone, and he knew that unleashing his anger on Signora Liguria had not been appropriate, but he couldn't stop. It was anger over his mother and the self-indulgent things Adelina had done all these years. When did he get to rush off to the city and dabble?

He gestured to a flat of mushrooms precariously balanced on a box of eggplant. "Make yourself useful. And use the brushes on the mushrooms, not water."

She glared at him for being reminded of such a well-established process for mushrooms and continued to fold napkins.

Just to see his sister again irritated him—the frivolous city girl. He shoved the mound of onions aside, wiped his eyes, and pulled the first bunch of celery into position. An "artist." Hell, first she painted tiny little squares that you could barely see, and then last year on canvases so enormous you couldn't possibly put them in a house. It was if she went out of her way to make sure that it would be impossible to make any money from anything she tried. And here he was, sous chef, learning sauces, and not a single dish he had invented had ever shown up on the menu—always only his father's recipes. Thankfully there were many recipes or they would've lost all their customers out of boredom. He was bored and frustrated—if anyone should leave it should be him, not Adelina, and certainly not their mother.

Adelina slapped down a napkin and walked to his elbow, lowering her voice. "Did they start fighting? You must've seen something."

"I'm a little busy here with my own life!" But he knew that was an exaggeration. He not only felt betrayed by his mother who would break up their family when his father was too old to look again (*47! Ancient!*), but he felt betrayed by love. Where was his love? His last relationship had fallen apart after little more than a year. He had gone to Rome for a culinary workshop and met Carlotta in a bistro. He brought her home to the village where it seemed all was well until she started talking about Rome again, complaining about what she called the "do-nothing" life in the village. First, they fought about it, then they spent the occasional weekend in Rome. When the time came to return to the village after yet another trip, she nonchalantly said, "You go ahead. I'll be back on Monday." The only thing that arrived on Monday was a letter suggesting a long-distance relationship.

"I need those eggplants cubed."

Adelina looked like she wanted to say something in retort, but took a deep breath and cut them with a speed that made Paolo turn to look briefly, but turn back to his sizzling onions and celery without speaking. When she brought the eggplants to Paolo, she set out capers, olives, red wine vinegar and a small container of sugar.

"*Caponata*?" She asked, though she knew the answer. Paolo gave her a tired nod. He wondered how many times he had prepped for this dish, and he tried to do the math of twice a week every week since he was eight years old.

He wouldn't move to Rome, become just one of the millions of sous chefs. He didn't like the noise, pollution, or traffic. And he didn't want to admit that there was a "cool factor" at work, putting him on edge, as if he would be discovered to be hopelessly rural and unhip. He had spent so much of his adult life complaining about the closed-in nature of village life, and yet when he finally went somewhere with endless possibilities, it had seemed frenetic and missing the quality of a few things done very well. He hadn't written back to Carlotta.

And though he vehemently defended his father, right now he felt trapped. Yoked in. The town he would live in had been chosen, his profession had been chosen, and he was too exhausted from the long hours of work to have any hobbies. He didn't play soccer on the weekends anymore; he didn't bike competitively or play an instrument. He was a cog in his father's machinery. He was not only not a self-made man, he was nothing more than an understudy to his father, which made him an unformed man.

He hadn't realized it until he had gone to the Liguria bakery. When he'd looked around the kitchen while the old woman scolded him, he was taken by the expansiveness of it, the high ceilings, the long table, so unlike the small kitchen at the *trattoria* where they cooked nearly back to back. And even if the baker had run off with his mother, Paolo felt that at least at the bakery there wouldn't be anyone forcing him to be behind the scene, ruling out any chances of advancement or creativity. Paolo wasn't partial to baked goods—he considered baking less manly than working with meat—but suddenly the clean-slate feeling he got from the room had gratified him. He wondered if his sister felt this way as she looked at a blank canvas. It was the newness of it, the idea that it could be his alone, that it was something that had never been tried by his father.

But it was foolishness, he knew: he was on his path. What would his father do when he got too old to cook? Sell the restaurant? Certainly not. Everything he learned, he learned so he could take over the business. He understood there was a legacy to be carried on, a grand tradition, and in these days of unemployment, he was lucky that he didn't have to leave his home and flounder in some unfamiliar city. So, as he watched his sister roasting the eggplant with more competence then he'd thought she had, he was particularly intrigued by the idea of the baker being gone and staying gone. His father and all the *trattoria's* patrons complained that there was no bread. What if he took over the bakery? Surely the old woman needed the income, and even if all she did was pay him a small wage, that's what he was receiving from the *trattoria* at this point anyway. It wasn't like his father would give the restaurant to someone else. And yet, he couldn't very well leave his father now, when everyone else had. Which meant they would continue to be a village without good bread.

***

Chef Dario Giordano knew that his feelings were changing by the way he chopped. The morning he awoke to find a note from his wife on her pillow beside him and her phone number disconnected, he had chopped the day's poultry with violent swings of the cleaver, leaving the chunks so ragged and misshapen that he made Paolo go back through the pile of meat to inspect it for bones. He had pounded the veal as if punishing it. Then, he was so distracted that he only chopped half of the vegetables for the minestrone. When Paolo noticed and demanded an explanation (which Dario had initially withheld for the sake of his own pride and, he convinced himself, to shield his son), Dario spilled the news—quickly, before the others arrived for work—and both of them chopped and sliced and bashed pots and pans on the stove, slammed doors of the cooler, and moved far more quickly than usual. At the end of the lunch rush, Dario sat at a small table outside the back door and absently cut up green beans. Just prior to dinner, he painstakingly skinned chestnuts with a small blade as if trying to extract a secret.

Today, returning from the greengrocer with ten small bunches of bay leaves and seeing his daughter's car in the drive, he sat despondently in his chair in the back garden, lacking the stamina to deal with Adelina. He was humiliated by the idea of his wife with an older man, and then he was just stumped by the puzzle of it. The only time he could imagine Rosa having gone out on him was one evening when she presented herself in a new dress—a garish purple that he had silently disliked—and when he'd said he didn't want to go out, she had pouted and gone out anyway. He had been quietly angry but couldn't stay hostile long—he never could. He treated her like a princess; treated his daughter that way too, and Paolo had once confided to him that people thought the two women were haughty and spoiled. Today he wondered what was worse: a cuckolded man who disdained and neglected his wife, or a cuckolded man who fêted his wife and still found that his best was lacking. He suspected it was the latter.

6

Bettina Liguria stood resolutely behind the table; her cane was hooked over her chair yards away. This morning she had laid the chocolate-making equipment across the table in neat rows and had washed them with great care, taking toothpicks to crevices, carefully polishing off dust and even more carefully cleaning off polish. It was too tender and respectful to be considered kitchen chores, and Bettina was energized by it. Her frustration over having spent her life on the vagaries of bread had mixed with the grief and anger of her son's betrayal to produce a determination that she knew was a little desperate and most likely unrealistic. She wasn't that strong anymore; her hands shook a little and her eyesight was not what it should be, but she had nothing to lose, and if Gretchen helped with the heavy lifting, and she spent her evenings writing letters to distant cousins and great-nieces to see if anyone wanted to join her, they might actually be able to reinvigorate the long dormant but (hopefully) unstoppable line of the Mistresses of Chocolate. That's what they had always called themselves, until circumstances had stopped them.

***

When Gretchen arrived at the bakery in the morning, Signora Liguria told her to move the iPhone altar to the end of the table and she brightly described to the American each of the chocolate molds, ladles, pans, collars for pieces that would stand tall.

Gretchen took notes but soon abandoned them as they were an interruption in the flow of Signora Liguria's instructions, the enchanting way that she described the chocolate, the heat, the single drop of a tincture that turned an ordinary truffle into what she called a thing of ecstasy. Gretchen smiled a little at the hubris of this woman who was usually curt and acerbic.

After noon, there was a knock on the door announcing the delivery of their supplies: bags of dark chocolate pastilles, quarts of cream, 10 pounds of butter, and 40 pounds of sugar, and Signora Liguria pressed another list into the driver's hands as soon as he had finished unloading the order. He looked around the kitchen with curiosity, but Signora Liguria flapped dismissive hands at him and quickly closed the door.

To Gretchen, the actions of the rest of the day seemed inexplicable. Signora Liguria whirled sugar and butter together until it turned into caramel; chocolate and cream were pulled off the fire just at the right time to turn into ganache. They wound up with a few scorched pans, and a second batch of caramel that turned, in what seemed an instant to Gretchen, into something resembling roof tiles, but there was far less wastage than when they were bakers. Signora Liguria, whose hands were now surprisingly steady and whose stamina on her feet had not been anything Gretchen had seen before, moved as if driven by deep memories, a subconscious reality that gave her movements a languid, flowing, effortless appearance and gave her face a dreamy quality.

7

1943

World War II had depleted the supply of chocolate, meat, clothing, firewood, a sense of safety, and finally, hope. Caterina and her 20-year-old daughter Maria—with baby Bettina in tow and her husband conscripted into the army—had nowhere to go and no way to get there.

Houses became empty at a moment's notice as villagers either fled or were officially called down from the hill and never heard from again. Flower gardens and window boxes died, dirt blew down the streets and caked the windows and doors. The village was nearly deserted, more dust devils and rust than a town, which made the confectionary's sculpted chocolate and decadent creams seem especially trivial.

Caterina had been one of the last villagers to remain as Mussolini, and the war that followed, flowed around but rarely marched up the hill to their village. At first, the family had stayed in their home because her husband, Stefano Bruno, was convinced that sanity would prevail, and the resistance would win. After all, they had established free zones and Partisan Republics, enclaves of freedom (though not peace) while surrounded by Italian Fascists; one of the largest free zones was in the hilly forests to the northeast of the village. The local men transported supplies to the partisans, hidden under the bed of donkey carts or deep in the straw of nesting chickens in their cages, some goods smuggled as ballast in boats plying the river that ran through the middle of the Free Zone to meet the Po. Last year, when the Germans had invaded the northern third of Italy, though, they were far more thorough than the Italian Fascists and, on the suspicion that the partisans were being helped, or perhaps to just send a signal to members of the Free Zone, they had rounded up Bettina's grandfather with another 20 of the village's men and shot them on the hillside.

***

With very little heating oil left, Caterina shivered though she was inside. She wore a woolen scarf tightly wrapped against the cold around her neck, a shawl over the top of her winter coat, and an apron over it all. Petite to begin with, she appeared to have shrunken inside her clothing; the gauntness of her face, as if chiseled, made her hazel eyes more piercing. Her long, dark hair sprouted out of her head like chaos, and she tried to hold it at bay with a wide band.

With painstaking movements, she carefully made a very small batch of confections (more careful than usual not to slop or waste it), and perhaps it was sorrow over her husband's death, the state of the world, or the pending demise of both her confectionary and her family that made her slowly savor each movement that was required to create a perfectly filled vanilla cream heart. Whatever the reason, the beauty of her motions captured the attention of a man looking through the back window from the alley and drove him to come inside.

Caterina jumped at the sudden intrusion but, upon seeing him, did not protest. Though he wore no insignia on his outside coat, Caterina could see his political affiliation: his coat was clean and well-fitting, and these days, one might possess a good coat, but it was assuredly crumpled and dusty from huddling in an air raid shelter, or sweat-stained and filthy from having survived interrogation, or, at the very least, out of place as a woman might be in a fox collar coat carrying an armload of dirty potatoes. This man was a member of the Fascistic Italian Social Republic, she thought, out of uniform, but at least his black hair and olive complexion made it obvious that he wasn't German. He was broad-shouldered, and he stooped low to come through the door and down the steps into the confectionary.

Caterina threw her shoulders back, stiffened her posture, and considered whether the molds she had just filled would set into ruined solid pieces or whether she had time to invert them to make shells.

"Good afternoon, Signore," she said as she flipped the molds over to drain. She thought about the butcher's knives she kept hidden throughout the shop and kitchen as she wiped her hands and took off her apron. Her dress was faded and mended in several places, but she adopted her most elegant attitude.

"May I show you our offerings?" She gestured toward the shop and when he nodded, she proceeded down the hallway, noticing that his step was very close behind hers. Though it was no guarantee, having him visible from the street through the shop windows might slightly increase her safety, she thought. Caterina gestured at the long glass case of chocolates that were intricate and shiny, but spread out on shelves that were nearly bare. When there is little money for food there is no money for chocolate. Sometimes she only sold a single piece in a day— when Father Domenico came by and pressed a coin on the counter that she suspected was mostly from charity.

Her visitor had looked around suspiciously when he had opened the door to the kitchen, only mildly interested in the workings, but seeing the chocolates, he lit up. "Signora! Beautiful!" He tipped his head to her in an acknowledgment of her abilities. "But you have so few left! Did another supply chief get here before me?" He leaned over the counter toward her. "Couldn't be the traitorous partisans buying your chocolates. They eat bugs and bark, at this point, don't they?"

"I wouldn't know what they eat, Signore," she said quietly.

"And you have gianduja? Hazelnuts?"

"Of course. Raspberry cream hearts, coffee ganache bells, gianduja-filled hazelnut truffles." He clasped his hands to his chest as if he had won something and ordered a dozen cream-filled hearts. Stepping toward the case then back like an indecisive boy who couldn't remember the number of coins in his pockets, he ordered two dozen ganache-filled bells and seemed to be restraining himself from buying all the truffles in the case. He described his mother's favorite hazelnut bonbon; he talked about his grandmother's hot chocolate after school.

Caterina boxed her chocolates up, pleased for the sale, accustomed to listening to customers' nostalgia, but not letting her guard down. Were there fascists at the bottom of the hill waiting to join him? Did he work with the men who had killed her husband?

When told she didn't have a box big enough for his order, he laughed. She stacked multiple small boxes up, laid them out, and, at his command, reshuffled their contents forward and back. When he didn't command her to reshuffle them a fourth time, she tied the boxes together and walked them out to his chauffeur who had driven a car with fascist flags to the front. When the chauffeur opened the trunk, Caterina nestled her boxes between a case of wine, four gold plates, two candelabras on their side, and a fur coat. He pressed a roll of bills into her hand while looking into her eyes with cold suspicion. She stood motionless until he had left and then, looking down at the money, she quickly hid it in her apron. This would keep her family in food for a month, though things had gotten so desperate that you didn't want anyone to know you had money or food: she had heard of families in other villages murdered for less.

Immediately putting her daughter Maria in charge of the store, Caterina took off her apron, put on another coat that she cinched with a belt, and secreted all but the smallest bills into the back of the deep, triangular cupboard. She set out to the greengrocer and the butcher shop, hoping they were still open this late in the afternoon, though there was almost nothing on the shelves and the bins at any hour. She had enough money to buy the entire ham that hung on the hook, but that would arouse suspicion. So, acting as if she was conflicted over spending on ham what for everyone else would have been their last coin, she ordered a small piece, then pretended that she was overcome with a desire to splurge and doubled the order. The butcher raised his eyebrows but quickly cut the pieces before she changed her mind. He looked down at the coins she put into his hand, but when she handed him one of the bills he looked askance at her: the bills were crisp and fairly new which meant they hadn't struggled their way through the grubby, hand-to-hand existence that everyone else lived. She curtly said her good-byes.

Caterina bought small bits of food in every place she could think of to give the appearance of people who could buy very little, and she returned to her rooms above the confectionary in between purchases to hide the food away.

The following week, the supply chief returned, inhaling deeply as he walked through the door of the shop, but when he saw that the shelves were as bare as when he had left, he slammed his hat on his thigh.

"Where are the chocolates?"

"I'm sorry, Signore," her daughter Maria stammered from behind the counter while she twisted a strand of dark hair, and a mottled red flushed across her cheeks. Knowing that a customer would be a rarity, Maria had been playing on the floor behind the display case with her baby Bettina, who was now asleep on a nest of blankets.

Caterina had stepped into the store from the back room at the sound of the bell on the door. It would not do to point out that he had given her enough money to replenish their supplies, though not to eat as well.

"I'm afraid, Signore, that there is no way for a delivery of chocolate to get through." She stood by Maria's side. "No sugar or vanilla." It was too dangerous to forage for hazelnuts in the woods. The shells of her filled chocolates were thinner than ever, not because of her skill but because of her thrift. She had a single vanilla pod left, and yesterday she had resigned herself to closing the business when her stock was sold out.

He was incredulous. "They're the nation's pride—Italian chocolates! And yours in particular." He reached into his inside coat pocket and drew out a piece of paper, doing some quick accounting. Caterina assumed he was selling her chocolates on the side. "This won't do." He drew closer to the display case. "I am a reasonable man," he said, pointing at his breastbone, "but my friends are not." He gestured outside. "And then there are the Germans," he said pointedly. "A standing order. I'll send a car around weekly."

"Then I will need an advance for supplies." Caterina shoved her hands into her apron pockets. Maria kept her trembling hands clasped behind her back, straddling sleeping Bettina.

The supply chief was stunned. Then he chuckled as he pulled an envelope of money from his breast pocket. "Captain Graziani." He extended his hand to her and when she took it, he pulled her forward until she was pressed against the display case. "Third cousin of Generale Graziani, head of the Army. If a single one of these bills winds up in a free zone…" He fanned the money out on the counter like a deck of cards, snapped his hat back on his head, and left the shop. It chilled Caterina to see what kind of hand she had just been dealt.

Maria stared, wide-eyed, at the money splayed on the counter. "Mamma, we have enough to leave!" She scooped up Bettina and held her close. "There's still a bus running to Genoa. We could go tonight! To America."

"This isn't enough for America. And there is nothing but war between here and the coast."

In the morning the phone rang, a surprising occurrence now, but it was a supply house informing her that Capt. Graziani had authorized a shipment. What did she need? The man on the other end of the line seemed nonplussed over the list.

When she hung up the phone, Caterina sat behind the barren chocolate case and considered her limited options: one simply did not say no to the Fascists, but being ostracized by the villagers as someone who was aiding and abetting was nearly as dangerous. There was a fine line between someone who could survive in times like this and someone who had become a collaborator.

***

In the ensuing days, the smell of chocolate and cream emanating from her kitchen drew to the alley behind the kitchen a cluster of little children hoping for food.

"Don't open the door!" Maria bounced her baby on her hip. "Our food is not for them, it's for us. Look how thin you are Mamma. Think about the baby. We don't owe it to them."

"We can't turn children away, Maria. We are nearly the only business left in town. Certainly the only one bringing in money from outside the village."

Maria looked around, exasperated. "What good does it do for *everyone* to be a little bit starving?"

Caterina gave her daughter a sad look, but gave the children small, broken pieces of chocolate, and started a large pot of soup with a hambone and a few vegetables. She took the first bowl to Fr. Domenico, pacing carefully down the hill with a small, lidded soup tureen. The next morning, the children were given broth with a carrot.

Caterina added extra milk to her dairy order and warmed it for the children, then slipped in a request for dried fruit that she made into bite-size tarts. The Mistress Chocolatier, *L'amante di Cioccolato*, fed the children every morning, swearing them to secrecy. But siblings and mothers arrived, then old women who traded tea, a faded doily, one of their last remaining silver spoons for a bowl of soup. A week later, the villagers announced that it was communal soup to be shared only with those who brought a turnip or a potato for it. The profits from the chocolates bought a little meat for the soup whenever it was available, and the butcher brought the last scraps himself before trudging downhill with a small suitcase and the goal of making it to Genoa.

As winter approached, the confectionary was one of the only places that could afford heat, so Caterina allowed orphans and the widow of the carpenter and her two children to make sleeping pallets in the kitchen. They rolled their blankets up in the morning to give her space to work, until it seemed the entire village stood outside the windows watching her make chocolates while they blew into their hands to keep warm. The widows of the other 20 men who had been executed doled out the soup in the evening and gave only cups of warm water during the day. The old cobbler, shaped like an egg with tiny feet, minced over every morning and sat outside to watch for strangers up to no good, though generally, the village was straight uphill from the main route and few—especially the very hungry—would make the climb on the off-chance of finding something. Whenever the Captain's chauffeur was due to arrive, the villagers removed all sign of themselves from the confectionary and hid in their root cellars.

Caterina went to Mass every day, confession three times a week, but Fr. Domenico, six feet tall with an oversized, bald head, was soon so poor that he was at the door every night for soup as well, and started leading prayers in the kitchen. The orders from the Captain grew in size and Caterina begrudgingly wondered where her chocolates were going, shipped to some elite club of brown shirts, and how much the Captain was profiting.

Maria continued her campaign: didn't they have enough to leave now? Couldn't they get to the coast and find a boat? How could she put strangers ahead of her kin? She seethed at her mother until the two resolved not to discuss it.

One morning, after the widows had shepherded everyone out for morning Mass and Caterina was alone in the kitchen, a tall, young man stepped from the darkened alcove next door and came straight into the kitchen. Seeing the rifle in his hand, Caterina stepped toward the butcher knife she kept hanging on the long table, but she reconsidered: the man was not in uniform, and he looked too poor to be a Fascist sympathizer. The way he respectfully regarded her made it clear that he wasn't a thief.

"Why are you still here?" He looked intently at her. He was tall and clear-eyed. A ragged sweater peeked up from the collar of his leather coat, but his neck was chapped above a thin scarf. His black hair, shaggy but clean, curled around the edges of his cap.

She gestured at the village hoping to sound nonchalant. "Who else will care for them?" Moving to the Free Zone wasn't possible: too many old women and children in an area that needed fighters. There were no fortifications around the village, no guns other than an old pistol the cobbler carried that Caterina doubted would fire. Standing in front of a man with a rifle, however, she realized that her protection of the children and the old in the village had made her feel a bit invincible.

How foolish—pretending to be strong instead of understanding her vulnerability. Something in his eyes made her want to be honest. She smoothed her apron and wondered about the condition of her hair. She challenged him quietly. "Why do you fight?"

He smiled a bit and his brown eyes lit up ever so slightly. "Who else will fight for them?"

8

He was the first man Caterina had seen who wasn't either a prowling Fascist or a skittering victim. He had a sad, but kind look. He was still strong. He was handsome and the breadth of his chest and his calm demeanor made her understand how tired she was. How much she missed her husband. She wanted to crawl inside this man's coat, to rub her cheeks across the wild stubble of his face, to gather up Maria and the baby and run away with him. She made a simpler offer. "Soup?"

His resolve flagged at the question, as if he suddenly remembered his hunger. "Yes, please." He laid his rifle on the long chocolate-making table and pulled off his dirt-stiffened gloves.

"Your husband…" he began. She held the lid of the soup pot in midair. "Your husband was very helpful to us. We were all very sorry…"

What could she say? There was a tragedy in every corner. Hers was not special. She dug the ladle into the bottom of the pot for chunks of meat and potatoes, held the bowl until his hands were over hers before she let go. She stood close to him as he ate, her head below his chin. It took willpower not to finger the buttons on his shirt or run her hands along the texture of his sweater and the firmness of his chest. He scraped the bowl clean and stepped back.

"How is it you have money to feed the village? We've heard about you and your stew pot, you know."

"I sell chocolates."

"To the Fascists."

She nodded her head and lifted her hands. "It seems they're the only ones with money."

He considered her situation for a moment. "You should have left."

He was right, of course. Caterina turned to the stove and poured him a mug of warm water. He sat and cupped his hands around it. She turned back to the stove and slipped a bit of chocolate into a copper pan, swirled milk into it. She never gave chocolate to anyone anymore, not the children, not even Maria. Every bit was needed for the Captain, but Caterina took his mug and threw the water into the sink, then poured in hot chocolate. The first sip made him close his eyes, shake his head. He pushed the mug back at her and stood. He tersely nodded his thanks and stepped toward the door.

"Would you like…" Caterina looked around the kitchen for something to delay his departure, or entice his return. "Please." He slipped out the door.

After the visit of the resistance fighter, Caterina slept with the others in the kitchen while Maria and her baby slept upstairs in the cold apartment. She told her daughter it was to keep their "guests" from turning on the ovens or stealing the sugar, but it was to keep a lookout for the man from the forest.

On the next moonless night, he returned. Edoardo Bianchi stepped over the sleeping widows and children and followed Caterina into the locked-up front of the store. Caterina sat him on a stool behind the chocolate case and gave him warm, wet cloths to wash his face and hands. He lingered over soup, sitting close to her though saying very little.

The next time, he came in the middle of the night, shaking with the cold, and she brought a blanket for him, wrapped his hands and neck in hot cloths. She tenderly wiped his cheeks until he covered her hand with his and leaned in to kiss her. Their gentle, brushing kiss turned hungry, and he pulled her onto his lap, kissing her with desperation, as if it could engender hope. The heat rose to Caterina's cheeks. Her attraction to him was beyond logic.

Her husband had been kind and quiet, unpresuming, which had seemed endearing until the war began and it was a time for bold men. Twenty village men against two Fascists—how could they have just stood there to be gunned down? Caterina hadn't realized how angry she was. The day of the execution, hours after the Fascists had left, she and Fr. Domenico were the first out to find the slain villagers; they were the two to organize the old men and wailing widows to dig graves. They held a quick Mass, but insisted the graves be left unmarked for fear the Fascists would think the villagers held them as heroes and kill more. Since her husband's death she had grown stronger and more resilient, though scarred. And her heart had changed as well. Burying her face in his hair, she was drawn to Edoardo for his strength, for his refusal to surrender.

"I couldn't drink the chocolate," he said, finally explaining his reaction during their first meeting. He stroked her hair and traced the line of her jaw with his finger. "It hurt to remember that life could be… delicious."

***

The chocolate orders continued to come in throughout the spring, and Caterina fed anyone who came to the door, including a nighttime cadre of resistance fighters. Edoardo was sometimes accompanied by a short man nearing his 60's whose stiff walk and swollen fingers showed the privations of the woods, and two young women who looked only a little older than Maria. After two months, she smuggled one of the young women—whose wide-eyed fear had turned into a bitter and suspicious glare—upstairs for a hot bath. The girl slid down in the water and wrapped her entire head in a towel so she could weep unseen.

One moonless evening Edoardo grew bold and entered the church as Mass was ending, slipping into the pew beside her.

Caterina scanned the villagers filing out of the church. "You shouldn't be here," she whispered ferociously. The priest had his back to her, replacing the chalice.

"Marry me," he said quietly.

"Edoardo! Someone could see you!"

"Marry me. Right now."

She pushed his head down and he laid it in her lap, wrapped his arm around her leg. Under the circumstances, she thought, it was foolish to make pledges of any kind. And yet, holding on to even the tiniest shred of happiness was an affirmation of life, wasn't it? Yes, she would gladly marry him.

She should get the priest's attention before he went into the sacristy, but that also might draw the attention of a villager, and even if the majority of them ate out of her kitchen these days, that didn't guarantee loyalty. She had no hold at all over the rest of the paltry congregation. Waiting as long as she dared, she cleared her throat and called out quietly for Fr. Domenico.

Caterina and Edoardo were married ten minutes later in the sacristy with all the doors locked and their voices lowered. Fr. Domenico was almost giddy with the chance to preside over a joyful event for a change. Immediately after, Edoardo slipped out the side door where it was particularly dark, and Caterina walked out the front door as if leaving an everyday Mass.

Back at the bakery, Edoardo tapped lightly on the glass door and Caterina quietly let him in, leading him again to the place behind the chocolate case, this time lying on a pallet of blankets she had built. They made love enveloped in the aroma of chocolate, hazelnuts, honey, and cream.

He arrived on the next moonless night, saddened. A compatriot had been shot during reconnaissance. The next time there was just a sliver of moon, Edoardo returned and their lovemaking was wild and daring.

When he returned two weeks later he looked shaken, a little sickly, with a sprained wrist and a slash on his forearm. She tended to him and their lovemaking wasn't hungry. It was solace. It was true.

It was a secret marriage, kept even from Maria. Despite their precautions though, Caterina grew anxious. She understood his absence when the moon was bright (although he had recently been taking more chances). But when the moon next waned, he didn't arrive. She paced the front of the store, wrapping and re-wrapping a shawl around her dress.

There was no sign of him the following week either. In desperation, she carried a pot of soup to the edge of the forest, but no one met her there and the silent woods made her stomach drop. There was only one explanation for her presence there, and the danger made her hurry back to the kitchen.

A month went by. He stumbled in. She was jubilant. They lay beside the chocolate cabinet, whispering. He told her of his childhood, quietly sang songs from when he was a boy, described his first dog, his mother's best cake, the way his father snored, and she laughed with her hand over her mouth. They talked of silly things, sweet memories, anything but the war.

At the beginning of the summer, the Captain accompanied his chauffeur for the standard pick-up. The sudden heat of the day made him remove his hat and swab his brow before entering the store. He inhaled the rich smell of chocolate, and Caterina saw him relax a bit in the cool shop. Gathering himself, he leaned over the counter with a glint in his eye.

"You have been chosen for something quite outstanding, Signora. Your chocolates are renowned. Thanks to me, they'll be included in a dinner for the highest-ranking members of the Party. There is talk of Mussolini himself. Imagine that, your chocolates gracing Il Duce's table."

From the inside pocket of his jacket he pulled out a six-inch *fasci*, the symbol of ancient Rome and the Fascists. He turned it over in his hands: a bundle of thin cylinders, strapped together, with a blade protruding under a lion's head.

"Two thousand, Signora. I want you to make 2,000 replicas. They'll be the talk of Rome. All the great leaders, with enough to ship to the German command." He was prideful, demonstrative. "The party is set for this Saturday."

Caterina sputtered a protest. "Four days? It can't be done! This is a very complex symbol, and for such a quantity…"

He pressed the flat of his hand on the glass counter. "This is not a request." He snapped his hat back on. "I have all the supply houses in Italy on standby for you," he chuckled. "My man will be here on Friday to pick up the finished pieces." Standing in the doorway, one hand on the doorknob, he gestured to the back of the store. "And there's a delivery for you out back. I warned you about my friends."

Once he had driven away, Caterina sat down dejectedly on a stool behind the counter and struggled with the mechanics of his demand. Two thousand *fasci* of this size could not be created in four days. It would take cauldrons of chocolate. Pick up on Friday, he had said. A delivery out back. She moved sullenly through her kitchen. All her boarders were still in hiding.

***

Generations of women in the village tell different stories of what happened when Caterina opened the back door. No one else had been there, but over the years, a series of families claimed to have been the first to arrive, to have borne witness.

Edoardo had been executed, his body thrown on a heap with the two women in his small cadre; the older man who completed their group was crumpled beside them as if a child had left a puzzle piece unplaced. Some say that Caterina's scream could be heard at the bottom of the hill, some said two villages over, that the scream banished cats. Others claim that she went mad and screamed for hours.

But what was true was that rather than her scream bringing assistance, everyone in the village dug deeper into their hiding places and she was left to run to the priest herself and run back, left alone to slide the other bodies off her beloved husband, lay him out on the cobblestones.

9

Fr. Domenico, with a booming voice, called to the villagers for assistance. Maria was shocked by the twisted grief on her mother's face and the pronouncement of her marriage, but could only watch as her mother lay next to Edoardo, stroking his cheeks and weeping, whispering to him.

Helped by the old cobbler, Maria and the priest hastily dug graves, lowered into them the shrouded girls whose age made Maria gasp. The priest enlisted others to assist with the rotund old man, while Caterina lay with her face buried in Edoardo's neck. But just like with the previous fatalities, there needed to be a quick burial in an unmarked grave. Fr. Domenico called quietly to Caterina, bent over her, and repeated himself in the hopes he could be heard through her sobbing. He finally shook her shoulder and spoke to her with decisiveness. It was time to let him go.

Caterina stayed on her knees through the prayers at the gravesite, her hands clasped fervently, crying into her knuckles. The villagers clustered on the other side of the grave and little girls pushed to the front to witness true love, true heartbreak. She stayed on her knees until the grave was full, and the villagers turned to the forest to find camouflage for the disturbed ground.

When they returned with branches and boughs, Caterina had stopped crying, and was standing. She turned to the priest, who had a large bough in his hand. Maria thought that the look on her face that wasn't of grief but of malevolence. Caterina clutched Fr. Domenico's bicep and looked up at him.

"We have to poison them," Caterina said with more ferocity and finality than anyone had ever seen her exhibit. Maria grabbed her by the elbow and turned her away from the others, hustled her down the street with Fr. Domenico on her other arm. Though they were surrounded by people who owed her mother their lives, informants earned enough to eat something other than communal soup. "Two thousand dead," Caterina hissed. "I want them dead, Father."

Caterina described the new order, both the quantity and imagery. Maria started to cry. Fr. Domenico shook his head first with disgust, and then with resignation.

"You have to make them. There is no choice here anymore," he said.

"Oh, I'll make them all right," Caterina growled. "How much rat poison do we have in this town? I want every morsel of it."

"And take the sin of 2,000 deaths on your soul?"

Caterina drew him close and narrowed her intense eyes. "Gladly."

Back in the kitchen, Maria tried to calm her. "We have to figure out how to get it done. We have to, don't we, Father?" She tried to quell the desperation in her voice.

"Two thousand?" Her mother paced in circles. "It would take a month or two to carve them all. It can't be done. I won't do it!"

"You have to!" Maria was afraid of what would happen if her mother took a stand. Despite the pain she felt at her mother's grief, she was stung by her mother's betrayal, though she wasn't sure whether it was from the shift of loyalties that her secret marriage denoted, or because she knew that she and her baby would be endangered by any protest by her mother.

Fr. Domenico, watching the two women in furious conference, interrupted. "Every able-bodied person will work with you." He shared a look with Maria. Her mother couldn't be allowed to fall into a stupor. "How do we do this, Caterina? Think of how we can do this. How much chocolate do we need?"

Maria watched her mother's expression shift to one of resolution, though her expression vacillated, as it would for days, between a brooding anger and a bloodless, vacant stupor. The first step in her mother's plan for revenge was the fabrication of the *facsi.*

"Two thousand pieces, 6 inches tall. Impossible to carve." Caterina paced. "Strands rolled around a central core…too painstaking."

Halfway through her calculations, she burst out weeping and put her face in her hands. "It can't be done. Run away, Maria. Take the baby and run. We'll all die. All of you," she shouted at the villagers clustered in the doorway, "run away! Maria, I'll give you every penny we have."

Maria bristled again at the thought of anyone knowing of their tiny stockpile of money. And yet this was the permission she had been waiting for, the opportunity to flee and make her way to America. But without her mother? The prospect made her feel faint.

Maria took her mother's hands and got inches from her face. "How would you have done it…before the war?" Maria shook her. "Pretend that it's…a crucifix."

"Send away for molds," Caterina said. She had two lion's head molds for marzipan, she explained, but they would have to grind the almonds from scratch. The molds made a dozen heads each, so 24, which would mean 125 operations and chilling them would take more than 30 hours. Compared to the rest of the operation though, the heads would be straightforward. They could make a solid mold and perhaps paint the ribbon with dark chocolate afterwards, and maybe even give the lion's head a little brush with white chocolate, but ordering a copper or brass mold for the stem could take months.

Maria knew that even with a mold, it was nearly impossible: their kitchen was so small that there weren't tables or workspace, and they would have to turn on refrigerators in every apartment and house in town (including the vacant ones), and probably transform all the root cellars from hiding places to cooling rooms. This couldn't be done. They'd all be killed.

"It's time for Mass, Caterina," the priest said, but when she raised darkly sinister eyes to him, he gathered the children, summoned Maria, and headed downhill to the church without her.

Caterina continued her calculations. Especially since she had so many amateurs working on it, she should add to the total to cover breakage and mistakes. Cut the ribbon sheathing and blade from fondant, then add the lion's head, assuming all the pieces could be made in parallel. Good God. Her stomach dropped. How big could the batches be? Divided between 4 days…she would need 24 people working around the clock. At best, they had 15 adults (only six of whom had decent eyesight) and a handful of children.

She circled back to her plan for revenge. How much rat poison per piece? Would it would integrate with the chocolate? How could she protect the villagers while they worked? And still, no solution to the question of the mold. Setting that question aside for a moment, she calculated the ocean of chocolate she would need.

Caterina was calling in her chocolate, sugar, almond, and butter order when the priest came back into the confectionary kitchen with what seemed to be a spring in his step. Maria followed him. His hands were behind his back and when he brought them forward they held candlesticks. Caterina looked up at him, then looked back at the candlesticks. Their shafts were the same reed pillar that made up the *fasci*.

"18 inches of stem. I have 20 of them in this size, another 6 that are larger. But all with the same pattern."

Caterina grabbed one out of his hands. "We can cut them. And they're brass. We'll have to cut them lengthwise to make a mold of half-rounds. Twenty of them, 18 inches long, that's 60 molds. Add for breakage, 2,100…we have to cycle them 35 times." She shook her head. This would still require more equipment, supplies and time than she had, but the key piece had been delivered. The plans for poison were temporarily driven from her mind. "You have saved us, Father."

Fr. Domenico looked down. "It's about time," he said quietly. Caterina was more the leader of the village than he was. He was sorry that, because the entire village relied on Caterina's strength and kindness, on her chocolates, she could not be allowed the time to grieve. He feared what she might become because of it. Already, she spoke of vengeance as if it was her salvation.

This war had proven that while his height made him appear to be an imposing man, he was not. He thought of the days he had heard wailing and done nothing, when he had prayed that he would not be called upon to shelter anyone: that was how great his fear had been. For years, he had felt that Mass had been essential or at least palliative, then when the war began, it was unanswered, and these days, inconsequential.

He mulled over Caterina's scheme. If there was a way he could take all the sin of the murders on himself, he would. But he couldn't sit by and let it be carried by Caterina's family. Through all his failings, all the times he didn't speak up, pretended to comply, this time he couldn't. And yet stopping her would amount to another failing, wouldn't it?

***

Caterina paced through the kitchen trying to imagine an assembly line for a process that had always been a quiet, two-person, specialized art. If they practiced with the small quantity of ingredients that Caterina already had, they could be ready for the supplies' arrival. She pointed at the floor as if drawing a schematic, muttering to herself, sat down on a stool with her head in her hands, and opened her eyes to see more villagers standing in the kitchen ready for assignment.

Fr. Domenico organized a posse of children and they foraged for tables to put in the confectionary, hauling in an odd assortment of workbenches, metal kitchen tables, and ornately carved dining tables. He and a couple of young boys dragged a cauldron from the laundry to the confectionary, and it took four of them to lift it onto the stove. They went house to house gathering trays, spatulas, long-handled spoons, and identifying any working refrigerator and spacious root cellar, while the cobbler sawed the candlesticks. Dissatisfied with the brass shafts' raggedy, hacksaw look, the cobbler scooped them into a sack and tottered to his shop to polish the edges smooth.

The oldest woman would watch the young children. The six widows with good eyesight would be her main workforce and would stand behind six tables in rows in the kitchen and be in charge of the chocolate shafts. Her apprentices, none of whom had ever worked with chocolate, clustered around her to learn the process: on a wire rack sitting on the tray, place the mold face up. Fill the molds to the top. Scrape the excess off and count to 60. Flip the molds over and give it two minutes to let most of the chocolate drain out. Flip them back and, making sure that the edges are smooth, transfer the molds to a tray and call for a child to run the tray to a root cellar. Scrape the drained chocolate—before it hardens—to the end of the tray and pour it back into another bowl. Call a child to run the chocolate back to the stove.

There weren't enough scrapers, but Caterina just had to raise hers into the air and a couple of adolescent boys (energized by the permission to break into houses) dashed off to find them. Ten shafts per tray was too many. Six shafts per tray, but the confectionary itself didn't have 10 trays and they would need 20. Two workers per table. They hauled another table into Caterina's root cellar and Maria instructed the older women in grinding the almonds for the marzipan. A trial run of the operation was sloppy and they shuffled tables, chose nearer root cellars, refined the process. The chocolate could not be piped—too slow. Ladling it in was sloppy. Caterina timed them with a stopwatch and walked between the tables, inspecting the shafts. Maria stood on a chair because of the height of the laundry cauldron, melting the chocolate over a water bath, but only Fr. Domenico was strong and tall enough to lift the buckets of chocolate and pour it into large measuring cups that were wrapped in hot towels to keep the chocolate liquified.

A teenage girl rang the long-handled school bell every five minutes to help the runners know when to return with the chilled shafts. When the first trays of shafts returned, they were set on a long table in the shop itself, and Caterina took a deep breath before she inverted the molds and tapped them lightly to get a half round of the shaft to drop out.

Most of the shafts were acceptable, though some had air bubbles and had to be thrown back for re-melting. But they were making progress. A child was stationed behind Caterina to catch the used molds, and the girl ran them to the sink for washing and a thorough dry.

"It's too slow. It's all too slow." Caterina was deflated.

Maria would have none of it. "Then stop wasting time on pessimism. We should probably assemble the two halves ourselves, so get at it." Caterina was surprised, then reenergized. Maria would pipe the puddle in which the shaft would stand while Caterina carefully painted a small line of chocolate to adhere the two half shafts together. They increased the size of the puddle. How much of a foot was really necessary? But Caterina was needed in the main room, so Maria took the task on herself, and the shafts started lining up. Fr. Domenico would have to melt the chocolate himself.

They worked at refining the process and producing what they could until there was no chocolate or marzipan left; the little children had fallen asleep in the corners or under their mother's table. It had taken all day to produce 100 finished *fasci*. No one had eaten. Caterina and Maria stood near the stove looking out at the work tables and reciting the process, too tired to remember it without correcting each other. It would have to do.

***

Later that night Maria was jolted awake when her mother grabbed her shoulders. Caterina was inches from her face, her eyes red and swollen from weeping. Her hair was a mass of tangles. Maria immediately turned toward baby Bettina and tucked her in more tightly, turned back to her mother with fear.

"I need you," her mother pleaded with a hiss. "You're the only one I trust. You have to find it. The poison, Maria. Only you."

"Mamma—" she whispered but Caterina shook Maria's shoulders, climbed into bed with her shoes and work apron on, wormed her way to a spot beneath her daughter's arm, and clutched her around the waist. She fell into a deep, exhausted sleep while Maria lay awake throughout the night.

In the morning, Maria walked to the church in a near panic. "She can't do this, Father! The poison. We'll all be killed."

He held her hands as they sat in a front pew. "It's doubtful it would work anyway. Il Duce has tasters for every dish and drink, everything."

"That's no consolation, Father! We'll be killed whether it works or not!"

The priest looked away. "She's right," he conceded, "We should be in charge of the rat poison. Do as she said and find every bit of it in the town. That way we can either destroy it or lock it up so there's no chance of her finding it. That's a beginning at least." And it left open the option of using it, he thought.

At noon, a large truck pulled into the alley behind the confectionary and deposited cases of chocolate, sacks of sugar, and wooden crates of almonds. Fr. Domenico shook his head. "It takes a month to get the Eucharist if it arrives at all, but this…overnight! Who did you say this man was?"

Maria bundled Bettina into an open kitchen drawer that served as a cradle and set out on her mission. She covered her dress with one of her husband's oversized shirts, tied a scarf over her mouth, and wore gloves as she rooted around under sinks and in basements. She commandeered a wooden crate and carefully put the boxes of poison into it, upright to prevent spilling it as she dragged it down the street.

It made her sick at heart, this mission, not just because of the pending horror of their discovery, but because in too many houses there were signs not of escape to a better country, but of people uprooted, surprised, snatched away with their soup on the table now molded and dry, their possessions flung and broken in a hunt for evidence that ultimately the Fascists didn't even need. Here was the apartment of her best childhood friend whose entire family disappeared in the night. The apartment of the schoolteacher, always proper, was immaculate and buttoned up, but Maria knew that while she had had her papers in order and her money in line, she had been too slow with her salute when stopped on the street, so they had forced her into the back of a truck and taken her away. Maria's task was voyeuristic and the forced intimacy of it saddened her: she was digging through places where husbands stashed secret liquor bottles, teenagers hid dirty magazines. She pushed aside broken things and old toys and the piled dung of rodents. Sometimes she found a few canned goods that had been stashed and lost. At first, she politely scraped her boots before coming into the houses and flats, but she quickly saw the foolishness of it, and that pained her as well.

On the last street before the downslope on the far side of the village, Maria pushed aside an old chair and a stack of boxes in a back shed. The building was dark and smelled slightly of urine. When her eyes adjusted to the light she flinched because there were two children huddled in a corner, a boy of about six with his hand over the mouth of his younger sister to keep her from crying. The three of them locked eyes, and Maria imagined that they all had the same hopeless and frightened look. She dropped her gloves and crouched in front of them.

"Are you alone?"

They didn't answer. Of course they were. Thin, dirty, clinging together. She didn't recognize them, but that wasn't unheard of: families en route to safety could be split up, parents killed, children told to run and hide. But if she brought them with her into the kitchen, they could be killed along with everyone else in this scheme. She supposed that was true of every day. Today, though, she had something to offer, and she wasn't going to leave them here.

"Come with me. I can help you."

They didn't move.

"I have soup. And warm beds."

She left the crate where she had found the children. She held the little girl's hand on the way back to the kitchen; her brother insisted on holding the girl's other hand, and he pulled them into corners and against the walls on the way. She wasn't going to tell him that they were safe. "They're not here now," she said to him. She explained the route to him, and as they slowly walked, she described the ingredients in the soup.

With the activity in the kitchen, Maria and the children entered almost unnoticed. She had them stand at the far end of the stove to stay out of the way while she scrubbed her hands and arms, her face, took off her husband's shirt. She gave them small amounts of warm water which they drank quickly, then a small cup of broth, which they gulped. After she had washed their faces and hands and set them on a pallet next to the stove, she gave them large bowls each and wrapped their shoulders in blankets. She put the carpenter's widow in charge of them for the time being, checked on her baby, donned her poison-gathering clothing, and returned to her task. One last street. There could be no failure in this.

The last house was the largest in the village—an exporter of olive oil who had fled six months ago. Maria sat down in the softly cushioned chair of the formal living room, her cellar-dirty dress and shoes in contrast, her rat-poison gloves thrown on the ornately inlaid side table. She had all the poison, from every house and flat in the village. She decided that the crate would be most inconspicuous in the garage of this house, and if discovered, why not cast aspersions on someone who was already gone? She set the crate in the garage, stashed the gloves behind it, scrubbed her hands and arms at a spigot, and headed with her shoulders slouched, her eyes downcast, to Fr. Domenico at the confectionary stove.

Caterina, making the first batch of fondant, looked at Maria with expectation and Maria nodded her confirmation. They had the poison.

"Father, I think I saw…more candlesticks." Maria gestured in the direction she had come. Fr. Domenico nodded and turned over the melting station to the tallest widow, retrieving a stool for her to stand on. He and Maria set out toward the garage of the big house.

"She won't be dissuaded," Maria said. "It's dangerous to handle: she could kill herself. Everyone in the kitchen. We can't put everyone in jeopardy."

The priest watched Maria become increasingly frantic. Caterina was a strong woman in normal times, he considered, but fueled by grief—she wouldn't stop. And unspoken was that neither of them had the strength to stop her. Fr. Domenico wasn't sure he wanted to try.

At the garage of the big house, Maria and Fr. Domenico contemplated the crate. What to do? They could set out decoys of empty boxes. No. They could lock it up, and Maria could say she didn't find any. But she had already affirmed her mother's question about it.

Fr. Domenico paced the garage, clenching and unclenching his large fists. Then he turned. "We need a substitute. A harmless substitute."

"She'll want it in the boxes."

"No," he said, warming to the topic. "The boxes are too suspicious. Why would anyone have 20 or 30 boxes of rat poison in a kitchen?"

"We could put it in a flour tin," Maria said.

Fr. Domenico nodded. "It looks like flour."

"You clearly are not a baker, Father."

Fr. Domenico continued to pace. "Plaster of Paris."

"No. It will clump when put into the chocolate."

"How do we know that rat poison won't?" he challenged.

"It doesn't matter. She has to believe that she has been successful so she will stop."

Fr. Domenico nodded, stroked his chin. They both knew food was so short that there wasn't any baking powder or soda in a reasonable quantity. "Soap is too flaky," the priest said. He paced. "Borax. There's plenty. She's not going to taste it. And if she comes to her senses we have a harmless tin on the shelf."

Maria clenched her fists and considered. There was plenty of it in the laundry that had just supplied the cauldron. Borax. Why not Borax? White, dusty, but not crystalline like salt or sugar. Not flaky. Harmless. "The trick will be to treat it like poison." He was right. She could ask for a large tin for flour, fill it, and deliver it to her mother with mock caution. They agreed that they should both continue to beg her to abandon the plan.

"Save us, Father. Save us from ourselves."

They both bent in silent prayer. If only he could.

10

The tin was procured, filled, wrapped in a cloth, and delivered at night with feigned secrecy.

That night, although they would be working around the clock, Maria took a break, gathered baby Bettina to her, and sat down on the floor with the two orphans. She pulled the little girl onto her lap, and the boy inched closer. They hadn't spoken yet, and she was in no hurry to push them. What was there to say in the face of all this? And she felt dangerously close to being an orphan herself: her father dead, her mother bent on this path of destruction. Before the war, she had been a young bride: her husband soon conscripted, still not heard from. Looking back on it, she was so much younger then, still her mother's daughter. Even after the birth of Bettina, her mother was still teaching her, still the wiser one. She hadn't seen how she relied on her mother, and she hadn't realized how confident she had been in her mother's solidity, how settled she was in her mother's shadow until her mother started on this suicidal plan. Maria knew that she had aged as she walked through the village looking for the poison.

***

By the following afternoon, the process had become smoother, and the clang of the brass shafts into a metal bucket became the sound of progress. The runners carried trays, washers stayed at their station, and the widow of the carpenter sang folk songs throughout the afternoon to mark the time. Caterina, in the root cellar, made a mound of ground almonds the width of the table, a well as large as a frying pan, and tipped in eggs and citrus, breaking the marzipan into melon-sized balls for others to knead. Late in the afternoon, both marzipan lion head trays, on their ninth recycling, were run to a refrigerator, but the location was forgotten and the children were sent out to locate them while the adults nervously took a coffee break.

They counted and recounted the growing number of shafts and lion heads.

Despite the progress, Caterina watched them with a sinking heart. It was too slow, there was too much wastage. The women were embarrassed by their inability; they were slopping too much chocolate down the sides of the molds. Too little was being returned for re-melting. Even with ten percent wastage they would fall short of their count. The tables were so close together that women were bumping into each other and there was still no room to roll out the fondant.

And Caterina's eyes were continually drawn to the flour tin of poison in the corner on the top shelf. It was certainly enough poison for her chocolates, and she imagined it sprinkling from the ceiling onto the growing lines of little shafts. As she stirred the chocolate she dreamt of it snowing onto the armies of the brown-shirts, a blizzard over Germany. Revenge soothed her pain. Her first husband's and Edoardo's murders had killed off belief not just in the probability of survival, but had called into question the reason for survival. Her daughter and granddaughter mattered tremendously, but there was a point at which even a mother understood that she was a woman with her own heart and life.

Maria brought her a cup of warm water to drink and Caterina

carried it to Edoardo's unmarked grave. She wanted to poison them in part so that she could be a member of the resistance, she thought, so that it would draw her nearer to him, continue his fight. To shrink from the task was to dishonor him. And yet if she did, the entire village could die, though that was a probability regardless of what she did. And there was little chance that it would be successful. Perhaps the poison was slow-acting and they would all die the next day so there would be no connection with the chocolates. The thought of them writhing in their beds gripped her. Die for Edoardo. Suffer as all of Europe was suffering. But what about the staff at the dinner? The innocent waiters who were given the leftovers? What of the village child here who snuck a piece?

The poison should go into the marzipan heads. It was the only place there was liquid to absorb it. She could attach all the heads herself, be very severe about keeping it separate from the rest of the operation. Regardless of what she did though, she needed to get Maria and Bettina far away from the village. She gently poured the remaining warm water from her mug onto Edoardo's grave above his head and stroked the mud it made as if it were his cheeks.

***

Upon her return to the confectionary, Caterina insisted that the marzipan heads be put on the glass counter in the storefront, and while they were being carefully laid out, she beckoned Maria to follow her upstairs into their apartment. She pulled the drawer out of the bureau in her bedroom, lifted a false bottom, and pulled out a stack of bills, smaller than either of them had hoped it would be, probably far too small to get Maria somewhere safe.

"Take this and go. I'm sorry I kept you this long."

Maria seized the bills and stuck them inside her blouse, furtively looking behind her and out the window to be sure they hadn't been seen. She should protest that she wouldn't leave without her mother, and a month ago she probably would have meant it. Today she looked down and said nothing. Caterina gripped her daughter's shoulder, then returned downstairs.

As much as she was glad for the money, there were now two things that posed a danger, Maria thought: the poisoning plan and a potential theft. Though she was needed downstairs, she opened a small quilt and hastily stitched the money between the layers, then used the blanket to strap Bettina to her back, where she carried her from then on. Now they were ready to dash any time the opportunity presented itself, but that afternoon, as she was mashing the vegetables from a small bowl of soup to spoon into Bettina's mouth, the little orphans tentatively carried their bowls and nestled in beside her. Maria sighed, understanding the cruelty she would inflict if she left these two behind, but there wasn't enough money for all four of them. She cursed the world under her breath, but kissed all the children on the top of their heads. She had a larger purpose now. She had to stay.

Despite the assembly line, there were some parts of the figures that only Caterina could create, and she spent hours rolling, then cutting, fondant until her hands were like claws. Fr. Domenico took her by the shoulders and insisted she lay down. The apartment upstairs had been opened so the workers could sleep in shifts. Maria watched warily: her mother had sequestered the lions' heads but the tin was in its place, seemingly unmoved.

***

They worked through the second night, though the clang of brass molds slowed. The third day they misplaced more trays, and Fr. Domenico ordered a siesta for all, including Caterina. Upon waking, Maria brewed strong coffee, but everyone working now regarded their goal as impossible. It was midnight on Thursday and the marzipan team was hours behind, but without additional molds, more workers wouldn't help, and the ribbons of fondant were initially too ragged and misshapen to use. Caterina thought about objecting to their lack of uniformity but then remembered that these were going to people she despised, so what difference did it make? In a world at war, who cared about mastery of craft? She dusted the work surface with powdered sugar and set thickness guides, nonetheless.

"Three bands," she called to the exhausted villagers. "Top, bottom, middle, four times around the shaft—just four times. Then one single band diagonally between each of them. Try not to pick them up!" The shafts were being marred by their warm hands. Caterina set bowls of cold water beside each worker. "Dip your hands! The water will make the ribbons adhere."

The chocolate work was finished late in the evening and all focus turned to the final assembly. The *fasci* stood in perfect rows, counted and recounted by Fr. Domenico.

By nine on Friday morning, Fr. Domenico shouted that they had reached 2,000. The women were jubilant, pulling off their kerchiefs with a sigh and hugging each other. The old cobbler and the priest danced in place and clapped. But when the tired workers clustered in the back of the kitchen and regarded the long tables that held the *fasci*, symbol of their destructions, one by one the villagers fell silent. Caterina was the glummest of all. She glanced up at the flour tin in its shroud.

Fr. Domenico saw Caterina's gloom. "Let us pray," he said with authority, and gestured toward the church. "Maria, you as well." This was Caterina's decision and he didn't want Maria to carry the sin of an accomplice.

But they were all complicit, no matter how you looked at it. If they killed the Fascists directly, was it still murder? Or was it being a soldier in the war? If they didn't, weren't they complicit in the deaths of thousands of civilians. And what about the complicity that brought the Fascists to power in the first place? Perhaps it wasn't his purpose or place to decide the morality of it. But he wouldn't pray for a coherent, understandable answer: that, too, was apparently not his purpose or place. He was lost. He was hollow.

***

When everyone had gone, Caterina retrieved the tin and set it with great solemnity on the table in front of the militia of *fasci*. She could sprinkle the poison on top of the marzipan heads and pack them all away herself. She could sprinkle it on every fifth one in the hopes of making it past the taster and taking out at least a few of the fascists.

And even though she was contemplating using them for murder, she had to acknowledge that the chocolate pieces were an achievement, considering they were made by amateurs in difficult circumstances. The fondant blades that she had cut were perfect. The ribbons were consistent enough and mostly smooth. Even the lions' heads were crisply formed.

On the other hand, she was not a soldier, and today her profession felt more foolish than when she created the most insipid little chocolate flowers. Yet when she packed the chocolates into makeshift cartons, ready for their pickup, and devoid of poison, she handled them gently, respectfully.

***

Fr. Domenico held a particularly long Mass that day, delivering a convoluted but passionate sermon on forgiveness, the challenges of morality, a litany that segued into pleas for guidance and safety, meandering stories that seemed to be half from the Bible and half from his own life, though regardless of source, they broke off in the middle and circled back to impassioned prayer. More unnerved than comforted by the service, the villagers slowly returned to the confectionary. Caterina had put the cartons of chocolates outside the shop in the shade, and when they stepped inside, Maria and Fr. Domenico immediately looked for the tin, replaced on its top shelf.

To Maria and Fr. Domenico, of equal surprise to the undisturbed tin, was the sight of the sterile kitchen. Caterina had packed away the tools of her trade: the cutters, knives, and pastry bags. She had removed all the flower and heart molds from their pegs on the wall, taken down the racks and scrapers. The long marble slab that had been on the table was found in pieces in front of the shop.

Caterina was just drying her hands when the villagers came in, and the only sign that it was a confectionary was a pot of hot chocolate warming on the stove. Cups had been set in rows on the first table and Caterina solemnly poured chocolate into each one, presenting it with murmured thanks to the widows, the children, the cobbler. Some devoured it hungrily; some couldn't bear to drink it because of its association with so much grief. Caterina took off her apron, set it on the table and went upstairs to sleep despite the cold.

A driver picked up the cases in the morning, but Capitano Graziani was not seen again. Fr. Domenico reasoned that perhaps he had moved on to impressing others with his source for caviar, brandy, Moroccan dates, or Chinese ginger. Maria and Fr. Domenico never asked Caterina about the tin nor questioned why it was that after they had skirted danger she had turned away from chocolate and her profession. Maria stood by with little Bettina in her arms the day her mother took down the sign from the shop door and scraped the word chocolate off the window with a razor blade.

Maria quietly tried to reason with her. The chocolates had fed an entire village—how were they going to eat now? The chocolates hadn't killed Edoardo, she said pointedly, but refrained from saying that he had been doomed from the start. Her mother mumbled something about love and purpose; about the optimism that is required for art, even the art of chocolate.

At this point in the war the question was not where to find money to buy things, it was where to find anything to buy. Fr. Domenico abandoned his collar, though not his calling to help others, and he and Maria went into the woods every morning foraging for food. Caterina looked after the children though she was too withdrawn to teach or entertain.

After the war, the village slowly came back to life. The sound of a truck straining to make it uphill was not the sound of the Captain or soldiers but of the vintner and the butcher. A new teacher arrived to reopen the school. Maria got a job in the newly-opened auto shop, and after mourning the confirmed death of her husband, settled into a quiet widowhood. Caterina sat alone in the little empty storefront, knitting things she sold now and then, and years later, she didn't protest when Bettina's marriage to the baker filled the kitchen with enormous ovens, sacks of flour, bins of yeast, and a smell more like beer than chocolate.

11

Present

As the days of Dario's wife's absence drew on, the clientele of the restaurant changed, as did the menu. At first the entrées were manly food: great bloody slabs of meat, *carpaccio*, lamb on the bone, things to gnaw on. The bar facing the kitchen and the prime tables just inside the canopy filled with middle-aged and elderly men who used Dario's tragedy as an excuse to drink in the middle of the day. The cigar smoke billowed out of the patio, and while Dario worked, the men grumbled commiseration and then, as the wine and brandy kicked in, growled about women in general. They spun stories of other desertions and betrayals, then started sliding into reports of men actually murdered by their wives until Paolo shushed them and pointed out that although the phalanx of men had driven most of the families away, there was still a small knot of women with their children in the back.

In the following days, the menu was comfort food, polenta, and cream soups. That was when the middle-aged women of the village, sometimes accompanied by their mothers, and the young women just slightly past prime marriage years, took the tables where everyone knew that the dappled sunlight would show them to best effect. They perched on the barstools with their legs crossed, their plunging necklines showing off their best jewelry, and their high heels hooked into the footrests. That Friday, salads and oysters were in great demand. The widowed owner of the cheese shop used her most dulcet tones to ask if Dario was cooking. Paolo was at first surprised (who else would be at the stove?), then he realized that she was the third woman ordering oysters—an aphrodisiac for men—as if sending a message to the kitchen. Paolo snatched the menu from her hands: how disrespectful to his mother, how calculating, and in some respects, how belittling to his father to be involved in this not-so-subtle innuendo. Like a man who insists that a shop girl model lingerie that he then sends to her, the obligation of it made it unseemly. And how rude to turn Paolo into the messenger. He abandoned the cordial chatter he usually kept up with his customers. They slurped their oysters, bounced their feet, and dreamily stared toward the kitchen. His father never turned to regard them, never registered the oysters' intent, but by the middle of the day, Paolo could see that his hands were swollen and bruised from prying the shells open.

By Monday of the second week, Dario was darting around the kitchen concocting an increasingly complex menu: baked sardines with garlic, lemon, and breadcrumbs; onions baked in their skins with capers; fish in a salt crust. He made his own sausages, though that was usually a task for last thing on Saturday; he baked sea bass in parchment and cannelloni with bitter greens. Paolo was happy for the variety, but complained that there was no room on the chalkboard for all that his father was creating, and that half of it would go bad since the village was too small to support the army of eaters for whom Dario was cooking.

Watching his father moving in the kitchen like a dervish, Paolo was convinced that his own future was getting further and further away from his control. His father was newly energized (through rage at Paolo's mother, or as a way of frenetically trying to avoid loneliness, Paolo wondered), which made Dario's retirement even less apt to be in the foreseeable future. Paolo ripped off his apron and hat.

"I'm going to look for bread."

His father didn't notice when he left.

Paolo wanted the bread baskets full, unobtrusive. Any mention of the breadbasket was, in part, a veiled reference to his father's cuckolding. But unless Paolo got in the car and drove for half an hour straight downhill and across the valley to the next village, there was no bread to be had. He walked straight toward the Liguria bakery with a step energized by purpose.

When he threw open the door and stepped down into the cool, dark, unnaturally quiet and cavernous bakery, it redoubled his resolve. Why shouldn't he become the baker? He clearly belonged in a kitchen; he had a way with food, and as long as the old man baker stayed away it could be his. He was relied upon at the restaurant to make all the crusts for meat pies and all the pasta. He liked the feel of flour and dough. Admittedly, he had never made bread. He had no recipe for bread and the village was accustomed to very high quality, but there had to be a way. He was unaccustomed to floundering around like this, to having options. His discontent had always been played with a single note.

He and the old woman had fought bitterly the last time they had spoken, so he saw no reason to ease into the conversation. "Is your son returning?"

Signora Liguria turned away from him. She had received a letter yesterday in which her son had insisted that she sell the business and send the money to an apartment in Rome where he had established himself with the chef's wife. That was a plan she had no intention of carrying out; others may think that her attempt to revive her chocolate legacy was foolhardy, but what else was she to do? Still, she didn't like being spoken to like that.

"What business is it of yours?"

"I will make the bread," Paolo declared, as much to himself as anyone.

Bettina threw her shoulders back. "Just waltz in here and take over, the way your mother waltzed in and took my son! We don't need you."

Gretchen stopped scraping chocolate from the rim of her fingernails, while listening with her phone. She rushed forward to Bettina. "Yes we do! I mean…let's not be hasty. Perhaps there's a way for everyone to…"

Paolo drew a big breath and paced through the bakery. "I could… rent the space from you. Maybe you get a cut of the total. You have a little money coming in, the village has bread again."

"This is a family business," Bettina said, though with less vehemence, "and you are not family."

"A different bread then. Bread that carries *my* name," Paolo proclaimed as he grasped the wide handle of an oven.

"We are making something else, something better."

"Signora, at least this plan will bring you income," Gretchen said softly to her.

Paolo and Bettina looked at her, then regarded each other tentatively. Paolo suggested a price. Bettina doubled it and demanded half of the proceeds. Paolo reduced his original offer by half and refused to give more than a quarter of the profits. Bettina scoffed at him and Paolo dismissively reminded her that he already had a job. She was the one in need of income, not him. He stormed out as he had stormed in. Gretchen looked crestfallen.

Bettina fumbled with her sleeve, then the front of her dress, flustered and anxious, knowing that his was a perfectly decent plan, but now that she had resolved to make chocolates, she didn't want to go backwards and fill the kitchen with the smell of yeast again. She brought down a cut-glass bottle of homemade *limoncello* and poured small glasses for herself and Gretchen. They would figure it out. It all had seemed insurmountable before. "At the turn-of-the-century," she said, "my great-grandmother, Delfina Conti Bruno, packed chocolate sculptures in oilcloth into boxes. Wooden boxes, custom-made." She lowered herself into her flowered chair. "She put them in hay inside larger boxes that were strapped to the underside of the wagon. To hide from the sun. And thieves. It often seemed insurmountable."

After World War II, the aroma of chocolate, hazelnuts, cream, and fudge disappeared from the village, banished as the smell of good things gone bad, of the brutal way the world could corrupt something sublime. Maria had worked whatever job was available: helping repair and reconstruct buildings, re-caning chairs, tending livestock. When some level of normalcy returned and a factory was opened five miles out of town, she rode the bus downhill every morning to work the assembly line and trudged back every evening.

Today Bettina drained her glass of *limoncello* and poured another for them both. Succeeding in chocolates again would be a tribute to her grandmother, a way to use the skills even though her mother had been denied them. It was an act of freedom, perhaps her last grand gesture; failure was not an option, despite how probable it seemed.

***

Dario, out for supplies between the lunch rush and dinner, passed children from the elementary school who were hand in hand, two by two, walking with their teacher down the lane and brightening the air with their chipper squawks. In the midst of their shrill joy though, Dario heard a more plaintive sound and lifted his head to see a woman, on her way home from the bakery, dodge into the lane 15 feet away from him, press her back against the stone wall of the building, and put her face in her hands to cry. This was the American with the beautiful eyes that he had seen on the barstool at his restaurant, eating his food with relish. Her chestnut hair fell over her hands, crying the way he wished he could. He hurried to her side.

"Signora," he raised his hand to comfort her but didn't touch her out of propriety.

She put her fists in front of her mouth, screwed her eyes tightly shut, then shook her head.

"It's okay," he said in halting English, and he put his palm flat against the stone wall. As if her more demonstrative crying gave him permission, tears welled in his eyes.

They stood very close, the man's broad chest slightly above her shoulder, his bulk shading her from the afternoon sun, and, to Gretchen, the quiet sound of his weeping was more comforting than anything she had heard in a long time. Unlike her ex-husband, who had tried to keep the grief at bay until it poured in and drowned him, this man surrendered to it. He smelled like his delicious food, only better. His black hair, which she had only seen mostly hidden within his chef's hat, now fell across his face and, appropriate or not, she wanted to bury her face in it. She put her cheek against his chest and wrapped her arms under his, across his broad back, mooring herself to him.

Dario leaned on the wall, his forearm against the stones, still shielding her, with her still clinging to him. He took his free arm and gathered her tightly against him. Her hair smelled like sugar and butter; her neck smelled of chocolate and he ran his hand up her back and his lips grazed her hair. He wanted to stay there: retribution for his wife, catharsis, a demonstration that he was alive and unbroken. Her arms around his back reminded him that he was still needed, that emotional hunger continued to exist. After decades of marriage, when he had become so accustomed to the little acts of understanding and care, when he had been married so long that he'd stopped wondering whether that care and understanding was sufficient, he had forgotten about emotional hunger, forgotten the thrill of discovery. He tilted her chin up and kissed her hungrily. She responded as if drinking him in, arching into him, and when it was clear that they could easily have slipped away somewhere to make love, she pulled back. Clutching his biceps to steady herself, she stepped a little sideways and wiped the tears from her face.

"I'm so sorry," she said quietly.

The din of the children was swallowed up by a library or church or classroom; she struggled to hear it as if it was the sound of receding danger. "My little boy…" She marshaled her strength to steady her breath and voice. "My son was recently…killed. In an accident."

It washed over her again. Gretchen had gone from a life where everything revolved around her son, to a life where all of that had disappeared. The trajectory of her life, the purpose, meaning, and structure of it had all been smashed like the bus. "You need a change of scene," her sister had said which Gretchen thought was absurd. She needed a time warp so she could hold her little boy on her lap and prevent him from getting on the bus. She had chosen Italy instead.

"*Mi dispiace tanto*," he said. "I'm sorry for your loss. The kiss? My…my fault." Dario dropped the arm that had held her and shook his head. What if they had been seen? In truth, he had watched her enjoy his food since her first day in the village; every night she seemed happier to arrive. Even when the restaurant was filled with angry old men, he made sure her barstool was free, that there was something on the menu that might delight her, though he did it secretly.

Gretchen tried to tidy her hair though it was not out of place, straighten her clothing though little had disturbed them. She apologized in English, then switched to Italian, while Dario apologized in Italian and switched to English. She motioned behind her to the village center— reason to move off, he assumed—while he spun a story about shopping. They started off in opposite directions, but then, realizing that they actually needed to go in the other direction, awkwardly passed one another again, but at arm's length. Mid-step, she stopped, turned and started back after him. He turned. "Dario, call me Dario."

She sheepishly bobbed her head, looked at the cobblestone lane, wiped the tears off her face again, and then threw her hands out as if unable to either express her gratitude in Italian or to suggest that things happen and sometimes one needs no explanation. "Gretchen."

12

Adelina put both hands flat on top of a large manila envelope that she had intercepted from the postal carrier, though it was addressed to her father. She sat at the long family table in the private courtyard behind the restaurant where she had spent much of her childhood shucking peas and trimming asparagus. It was one of her favorite places. The grapevines over the trellis, the aromatic kitchen garden along the walls, the smell of basil in the sun, the contrast of stone and moss, the little fountain that was a gentle accompaniment, counterpoint to the large fountain in the square in front of the restaurant. The back courtyard was a sanctuary: they had gathered there to report on the day at school, to sit with her father before he had to go back into the kitchen for the dinner rush, to inhale the delicious smells and to see her mother's eyes filled with a contented, tired pride. (But how contented had she been, really? Adelina wondered.) She had thought her parents would always be here; that she and Paolo would bring their own children here and find her parents side-by-side, their feet up after a good day's work, happy and together. It was a place filled with intimacy, privacy and admiration, wasn't it? That expectation made it all the more difficult to be sitting here looking at divorce papers sent by her mother who hadn't sent an explanation to Adelina or Paolo, or even a goodbye.

Equally as painful was the fact that her boyfriend hadn't called to ask about her departure, even once, let alone to plead with her to return, or, upon hearing her renewed outrage at his latest philandering, announce that he would mend his wandering ways. The soft comfort of the courtyard was now mixed with Adelina's anger at her mother for the callous way that she was handling all of this, as well as Adelina's chagrin for having initially laid all the blame at her father's feet. She had had the envelope for several days now and yesterday had carefully opened it in the hopes that she could find a return address or new phone number for her mother, so she could call her or drive there and talk some sense into her.

Paolo's news earlier in the day about the bakery hadn't been comforting to Adelina either. He had been pacing the courtyard, excited and secretive, energized by the idea, as if the scandalous departure of their mother and the baker was an opportunity instead of a tragedy. And his excitement annoyed her. He was in line to inherit the restaurant, but instead he strutted around the garden complaining that he needed something of his own. He had no idea how few people have something at all, let alone something unique. She'd thought her art was her own, and it turned out that she didn't necessarily have anything unique there either. A boyfriend who shared himself with others, a talent that didn't really stand out—that was what she had, and it amounted to very little. Paolo would probably borrow the money for the bakery from their father, so not only deserting him but using their father's money to finance his own desertion. The thought made her livid, and she decided that she would tell him so. Since he wasn't at work, Adelina assumed that he was at this bakery of his, so she set a big rock on top of the envelope to prevent it from blowing away and headed toward the bakery.

The front door was locked, the curtains drawn across the windows, so she tried the little door beside the shop and stepped into the alley.

She knocked on the door and then let herself in, propelled by her agitation. But when she got into the kitchen, there was no sign of her brother, just Signora Liguria, whom she hadn't seen in years. The old woman was bent over the stove, stirring something as if the spoon took all her strength.

Bettina flinched when Adelina said hello, turned slightly, then moved back to the pan and tried to lift it. It wobbled and slammed back on the burner with a clang.

"Careful! Let me help you." Adelina pushed up her sleeves as she quickly walked toward the stove, grabbed a towel, and picked up the pan with both hands.

"On the marble there," Bettina said, gesturing to the slabs on the end of the long table. She was a little shaken to see that she no longer had the strength to lift even an 8-quart pan. "In a ribbon."

Adelina slowly poured the molten chocolate onto the table and smiled as it puddled and became a long, hot river. Her gestures were smooth, and the pour was even; when she reached the end of the table she pivoted effortlessly, grabbed a rubber spatula from the counter and created a smaller, separate ribbon, scraping the pan clean. Standing at its head, she set her fingers on the edge of the long table. "That's a beautiful thing."

Bettina gripped the offset knife, then decided to turn it over to Adelina instead. "Go, go, smooth it to an even, thin layer. Quickly, before it sets." Adelina grabbed the knife and began the task. Bettina watched her carefully. She inspected the girl's work, bending at the side of the table to check the thickness, peering at it for pocks and holes.

"What's next?" Adelina asked.

"Wash your hands, girl."

Adelina jumped to it.

"Now take this bowl of cashew pieces. We do a strip of each along the width. Cashews, then almonds, raisins and sugared cranberries, then sugared walnuts. Anything left we jumble all together and put at the very end." Adelina walked the length of the table around the side, back up again, bending, touching a cashew bit to make it lay down, adding a sprinkle of sugared walnuts in a slightly bald patch.

Even though Adelina was moving quickly, Bettina noticed that there was a fluidity to her movements, a consistency that was essential for chocolate. But what struck Bettina most was the look on the girl's face. It seemed to her that she was not working *on* the chocolate as much as she was in communion *with* it.

Bettina realized that in her struggle to save the batch of chocolate she hadn't bothered to ask the girl her name.

"Adelina."

"Have you ever worked with chocolate before?" Either education or inspiration, there had to be a reason the girl was this good.

"No, but I grew up in the restaurant. I'm Dario Giordano's daughter. It's good to see you again, Signora Liguria."

At the sound of Adelina's last name, Bettina stiffened.

"I...was looking for my brother." Adelina looked down at the chocolates again. "Thank you for letting me help you." She inhaled and smiled.

Signora Liguria's stamped her cane and turned her back on Adelina. She should've recognized her: Bettina had watched her grow up, after all. At first, Adelina had been a timid and forgotten child, but Bettina had stopped watching her when she hit adolescence because it was inevitable—she would flit after the first shark with hair gel and wind up ruined. That she moved away at least shielded the village from her lasciviousness, which was a blessing for her mother (who at this point clearly didn't deserve any sort of blessings at all). The few times Adelina had come back to the village, Bettina recalled a lot of shouting, the girl sharp and bitter, done up in gaudy city clothing. Most times when she left, it was in a rage, hurling luggage and purses. The whole village could hear her tires squeal as she plummeted downhill.

But watching her with the chocolate—that was a different story. She was soft, attentive, attuned. Bettina knew what she was witnessing when she watched Adelina pouring the ribbon of chocolate: she had the touch, the love that was required to be a chocolatier. But the idea of someone from that immoral family becoming the chocolatier in her business was more than she could bear. Which was the biggest betrayal? Spending her life on bread with her heritage boxed up and hidden?

Raising a son who left her alone and penniless? Or turning the gift of chocolate over to an outsider? At least Adelina was Italian and from the village. Someone who might help after the American went home. Despite what she thought of her, this girl might help her avoid the widows' park bench.

"Your brother isn't here." Bettina lowered herself with weariness into her flowered chair. Love drove it all, didn't it? Love of heritage, love of rebellion. Love of purpose, craft and mastery, food and the senses. Of freedom. Family. Even the love of responsibility and obligation. But in too many cases, the flight of love, the heartbreak, the broken vow, the love of self that represses others; love that couldn't be, or should not be allowed.

Adelina regarded the long table, the molds and tools that were laid out in neat rows on the counters, even on the open oven doors.

"Did you ever hear how chocolate came into my family?" Bettina offered her the opposite flowered chair. "Make us espresso. Come and sit."

13

1863

Chocolate had first been brought into the family by Bettina's great-great-grandmother, Gemma Costa, born in 1855, here in the village. In truth, her great-great-grandmother hadn't been a Costa, she was a seven-year-old girl named Lidia whose life had unraveled when her mother died of the flu in 1862.

Lidia's father had received some compensation for having his hand crushed in a public works project, and he seemed to be in a hurry to find out whether his liver or his money would desert him first. During the day, as her drunken father slept, Lidia did as her mother had done and dug through his pockets for food money. At night, she ran through the alleyways to stay out of his reach: he threw things when he was drunk. Lidia slept in half a dozen basement cubbyholes and forgotten closets around the village that she lined with her mother's coats for bedding. Late afternoons when he woke up, her father assumed that missing food or chairs out of place were from a late-night meal he must have had. But where was Lidia? Because her father never saw her, it took only a few drinks back at the bar before he railed about his conviction that she had been kidnapped and tried to enlist the help of the bar patrons in the search, though he was so drunk by then that in the morning, he didn't remember any part of the story of the kidnapping or the search party, and assumed she was at school, even when the summer recess had started weeks ago.

Most of the women in the village secretly gave her food or a bath and invited her in for a chance to do her homework during the school year. They whispered among themselves about her, sometimes outside church after services, sometimes at the greengrocer, asking where she had been spotted, who had seen a glimpse of her as she scurried around town. They had threatened their men not to betray the little girl, and so every evening, the men placidly listened to her father's overwrought and slurred theories about her kidnapping and tolerated his denunciations when they declined to join the search.

One night, during a particularly heavy downpour, her father had woven through the village calling for her in a rage as people shouted at him from their windows. The rain sluiced off the roofs, gushed through drainage pipes and made the as-yet-unpaved road down to the church a muddy torrent. The rain flooded Lidia out of one of her hiding places, and she scrambled toward another one, but it was half-filled with debris from the rain. She cried over the way it had defiled her mother's coat, but her father's voice was close behind her. She ducked into a little cubbyhole that had previously been too high for her to see. It even had a door she could close behind her.

She wanted to be another child. Someone else's child. If she was unrecognizable, pretended not to be his child, maybe he would walk by her and keep walking, look for someone else to shout at and throw against the wall. Trembling inside the cubbyhole, Lidia fell asleep.

Just before dawn, a door on the back end of the cubbyhole opened and someone reached in looking for the cream. Then the door on her other side opened as well, and the milkman jumped back at the sight of her. Given the choice of the two directions, she lunged toward the smell of chocolate and tumbled into the confectionary. Men in aprons put down their spoons and strode toward her shouting, but they parted as Signora Costa, a tall, childless widow, stepped forward while tying her own apron. She looked down at Lidia and smiled sadly. Signora Costa had often lain awake worrying about whether the drunkard had found her; one night she had put on boots and cinched a coat over her nightgown to be ready if she heard the child shriek.

This morning, she tenderly stroked the girl's head. "And who do we have here? Lidia?"

The girl held her head high. "No! I am Gemma."

The woman was impressed. "Well, Gemma, you look remarkably like the youngest daughter of my late husband's sister. You look like Gemma Costa."

Lidia held very still.

"Is that who you are? Gemma Costa?"

Lidia nodded tentatively.

"Well, since you are family, let's get you cleaned up and get some food in you." She turned to her staff. "Proceed! This is not a puppet show!"

From then on, the girl was referred to as Gemma Costa by all the adults of the town and, though the priest wouldn't join the collusion, he was quiet about the truth until two months later, when the girl's drunken father stepped off the edge of the plaza and fell straight downhill to his death.

***

Gemma and her adopted mother at first fumbled around their life, as Signora Costa was inexperienced with motherhood and Gemma was unaccustomed to safety. Together, however, they indulged the chocolate. To Gemma, chocolate was the smell of rescue, of safety, the aroma of her definition. Her studies felt like gratitude, and together they spent evenings marveling at how thin Signora Costa could make chocolate bowls that would still hold their shape.

As a skilled teenager, Gemma built a crèche of chocolate, a model ship, an imaginary cathedral that was intricately carved with buttresses and stained-glass windows of spun sugar. By the time Signora Costa was an old woman and Gemma had taken over the business, the confectionary was responsible for half of the shipments in and three quarters of the shipments out of the village.

And a number of the shipments involved rare spices—small boxes bearing stamps of Indonesia, and even smaller parcels from parts of the newly colonized Africa—until the spice trader decided that rather than simply sending them in the mail he would visit his intriguing customer. After meeting the 18-year-old Gemma, he began arriving unexpectedly with samples of obscure and potent spices. The vendor, Alfonso Conti, traded in his wanderlust after years on the road and sea, won her heart, and became father to their five children. They lost their two boys to childhood illnesses, and one of their daughters died after a long bout of influenza which sent Gemma to her bed with nightmares of her own mother's death. Both of her remaining girls were devoted to her, though only one of them, Delfina, born in 1885, had the touch that made Gemma know that she was a true chocolatier.

Delfina's chocolates were a wonder: after two generations of women chocolatiers in the village, no one was surprised that the little morsels caused big men's eyes to water or that the dogs barked at her carvings of rabbits.

But it was her sister, Anya, who changed what it meant to be a Conti. She was too clumsy for chocolate carvings, too impatient for caramel, disinterested in making the little curlicue that designated a maple cream as opposed to a ganache-filled candy. Routine chafed Anya—repetitive motions, a regimen of chores, the unchanging vista, the same vendors arriving on their appointed days. Not like her sister, Delfina, who could make the walls of filled chocolates the exact same thickness over multiple molds and multiple weeks. To Anya, the work itself seemed second best: represent the flower but not grow it; mimic dogs, cats, sheep in lifeless chocolate; create fake crowns, love tokens, medallions. Genuine life, with more than one aroma, multicolored and unpredictable, seemed to be just outside her reach. But she persevered with the dreaded chocolate—it was the family business after all—while a part of her mind floated beyond the horizon.

The last born—and so the one most free—Anya had inherited her father's wanderlust. As a little girl, she would venture so far into the woods, so far out on the promontories or downhill halfway to another village, that her mother, in her alarm, decreed that certain groves of trees were off limits, that there would be punishments if she passed the large rock before the forest. Her father, though, seemed to delight in having passed on what he secretly considered one of the best parts of himself—his sense of adventure—and he would turn up unexpectedly (even when she was certain that she was on a never-before-discovered path), scoop her up, hold her close, and chuckle.

"Are you off on a quest, little one? Chasing the finest anise stars? Or the galangal root?" her father would question, more of a challenge than a query, pronouncing the name of the spice as if it were a monster. No simple herbs or salt for her, he would say, his voice rising from fatigue to a bright note: she was the true adventurer.

"The galangal," she would chirp.

"Hunting the zedoary, like the ginger and turmeric for which the world pays handsomely. Is that your treasure?"

They would chant it together coming back from her escape into the woods. "Galangal and zedoary, galangal and zedoary."

As they trudged back uphill or through the forest, Alfonso would hold her on his hip and spin wild stories of his life on the spice trail: staffs of cinnamon so big they were mistaken for rigging; pepper pods jostling in bags that spooked horses; the air in a town infused with the smell of his clove shipment two days before his arrival.

Anya clung to the stories of her father's adventures, even when the young men who courted her laughed at her desire to see the world. To Gemma's disappointment, Anya refused all marriage proposals and hardly noticed when they stopped being offered.

In the early summer of her 20th birthday, Anya again talked about striking out on her own, a topic that started with a wistful tone and, after meeting fierce resistance from her mother, turned acerbic, then angry. As she watched the daylight fading, she scrubbed the molds. It was 1908—a new century—and things were changing! Her mother gave her a stern glance and pushed her aside at the sink.

"Young ladies do not travel alone, and we're not a family that can afford to send you on a 'grand tour' of Europe. Besides," she said, unwilling to start an argument, "we're going on holiday now!" They were heading out right after the kitchen was given its annual scrub (the only time it was closed other than on Holy Days), to spend four days in a beach town in a sheltered cove on the Mediterranean coast where they went every year. "Plenty of adventure," Gemma said. And this time all the cousins would be there: people they hadn't seen in years. It was very exciting, according to her mother.

The prospect of the family holiday could usually keep Anya whistling through her chores, but this year, Anya packed their picnics and clothing with little glee. She had never gone anywhere else, especially anywhere alone, or to a place that a member of her family had not already been. All the rough edges were smoothed off for the ladies; the well-worn path was as far as anyone could imagine or permit her to go. Wedging salami and her father's favorite cookies into the basket, she could barely imagine it either.

***

The harbor was horseshoe-shaped, two rocky outcroppings framing the entrance. A small, gingerbread-style guesthouse offered meals and rented out the small sailboats that were tied up among the yachts at a row of six docks. Fire pits dotted the sand, and there was room for tents, though the Conti family stayed in the guesthouse now that the girls were grown. The first thing Anya would do after getting out of the taxi that brought them from the bus (that ferried them from the train that they caught after a bus from the village) was walk straight down to the end of the first dock that was closest to the open water and let herself become mesmerized by the surf crashing just outside the harbor.

As a little girl, Anya would spend all day in her bathing suit running down the beach kicking at the sea foam. More than once she had to be rescued from a rock shelf where the tide had trapped her. For her 12th birthday, Alfonso had paid for both of them to take sailing lessons from the grandson of the innkeeper, despite Gemma's disapproval and Delfina's prim disinterest. It became Anya's favorite part of the year:

father and daughter, learning together, competing a bit, friends and family at once. Was Anya fearless because she was so young or because she was Alfonso's daughter? She thought nothing of capsizing when she tacked too severely, of lunging across the front of the boat to grab a wayward line; or of heading into significant wind, even sailing in the rain. Delfina seemed happiest when pulling a tray of chocolates from the cold cupboard, but seemed overheated and bored by the seaside. Anya never lit up like this when they were in the mountains, even after having run through the forest.

In the evening of every summer after her 12th birthday, the old man who ran the inn taught Anya and her father to read nautical charts, in exchange for stories of Alfonso's transport business. Both men put their feet on the table, a glass of port each, as the innkeeper told of a storm that shot the rigging of a schooner through the front windows of the inn, and Alfonso described the routes where teams of oxen were best used, the location of an ingenious shortcut that had been found by his dog, the plains where he had driven his four-horse wagon in a dust storm, the winter he nearly lost two fingers to frostbite and had still delivered on time. Anya and her father smiled at each other across the polished wooden table in the sitting room. It was camaraderie devoid of all discord, especially now that she had bathed, put up her hair the way that Gemma liked it, and changed into a modest lace blouse and a straight black skirt. She looked trim, healthy, and obedient, though both she and her father knew without saying that the last attribute could turn in a second.

The summer she was 16, Anya learned to use the compass and her father insisted she learn the astrolabe, though Gemma shook her head at the foolish waste of time. "We're seeing if it can be…made into a replica," Anya fibbed brightly. "A chocolate replica, Mamma." Alfonso scowled but noticed that her comment eased the tension.

This year, though, was a long weekend with Alfonso's extended family. With great jubilance, backslapping, and exclamations over the growth of children, four branches of the Conti family held a chaotic bonfire. Third cousins had come down from Romania, pitched their tents in the sand, cooked mutton and vegetables in soot-blackened cauldrons, and drank late into the night. Cousins who had migrated north spent their days fishing in the surf, and they shared their catch, though not their stories as they retired early each night. An older cousin, Luigi, who hadn't been seen in years, arrived with his second wife, a Persian whose nose ring and bright fabrics contrasted with Gemma's tight white dress with a high collar. But the woman was honored among them because Luigi had worked in the family spice business, established by Alfonso's great-grandfather, when it still involved camels and long treks over the desert that were followed by dangerous sea voyages. Alfonso and Luigi talked long into the night, quietly trying to piece together the whereabouts of people they knew, discussing the developments in towns along the routes they each had taken. Anya thought her father looked particularly sad after talking with Luigi: he walked the beach in the moonlight, downcast. Following behind him, Anya wondered whether he regretted his decision to settle down, work in his wife's confectionary, and give up the road. It seemed a poor exchange to her.

On the third day of festivities, when the men had taken over the cooking and started a crab boil on the beach, a boat moved at a steady pace into the harbor. With a bright brass horn that pierced the quiet morning, the boat turned in a tight circle that threw up a frothy wake, a turn radius tighter than anyone in the harbor had ever seen. What sort of boat was this? It had no jib to tack, no sail at all. It had no oars, and it didn't even seem to have a belching chimney for steam. It seemed only half completed, a boat with no visible signs of propulsion.

Pointing and calling to one another, boys playing ball in the sand ran forward; grandparents and fathers cautiously walked up the beach and onto the dock. With a final short, blast of the horn, the boat circled once again; the onlookers called for the rest of their families to join them, and the boat pulled toward the dock. Just before reaching the pilings—where the dock was thick with workers away from their tasks, women with parasols, and fathers with young sons—it cut its noisy engines and glided beside the crowd. A young dockhand tied them fast.

A tall young man stepped out from the pilothouse in very dapper dress: shiny buttons and a tight vest, a shirt that had been pressed, solid

Wellingtons that were well-fitting and cinched at the calf. He was taller than anyone on the dock, with thick blond hair and ice blue eyes. "A fine good afternoon to you all," he said with a theatrical flourish. "Let me introduce you to the latest in the exciting and ever-changing world of marine transportation!" He threw his hands up like a circus barker and walked the deck. "A steel hull outfitted with an 80 HP engine from," he leaned toward the crowd to heighten their anticipation, "an automobile! Ladies and gentlemen, a gasoline-powered boat! Please, step aboard and see this remarkable new technology."

He lifted the back hatch. The men pushed forward and looked down at the engine. "The British International Race was just held, my friends. Gas-powered boats from seven nations littered the sea with contestants…new innovations in every craft."

Anya's father and Uncle Luigi walked to the dock and, as assertively as they could without causing offense, pushed their way forward, Anya following with her hand gripping the back of her father's coat. The three of them stepped aboard, walking around to the far side where the young boat-owner stood holding a midship hatch door. They looked down, then looked at each other. Imagine what their trade could've been with a boat like this. Alfonso walked carefully through the boat appraising the metalwork, the configuration of the pilothouse and ship wheel. The salesman secured the hatch door open and strode toward Luigi and Alfonso. Luigi stepped forward and, finally close enough to see the young man's eyes, stopped in his tracks, ran a hand through his thick black hair. "Johan?"

The young man dropped his circus barker air and his eyes widened.

"I'm Luigi…Conti. Your father."

Both Alfonso and Anya stood frozen with surprise as Luigi rushed forward and embraced his son, who was so much taller than his father that the little Italian was almost engulfed. Alfonso knew of but had never met Luigi's illegitimate son. Johan looked to Alfonso just like a picture Luigi had of him as a little boy, a precious item that Luigi kept in a wooden box with his mother's rosary and the birth certificates of his daughters.

Luigi looked just like the one picture that Johan had of his father, given to him by his mother just a month before her death last year. Then Johan realized that he had a crowd on the dock and a job to do. "Dinner? We'll talk then."

He resumed his showman demeanor. "Gentlemen!" Johan waved an open hand across the dashboard: a compass, several gauges for fuel and battery, and an accelerator lever like one they had never seen. He was quickly joined by the men who had crouched by the motor. Johan stepped into the middle of the crowd.

"One person can pilot this entire boat," he said to the crowd, who murmured and checked each other's faces to see who believed him. "A boat so easy to operate," he said, "it could even be piloted by a woman!" He started laughing with the men in his audience.

"Glad to hear it." A young woman stepped forward. "Please show me how."

14

Anya reddened when Johan chuckled and looked to see if the rest of the crowd was sharing his joke. "Oh, now sweetheart, it's just a figure of speech. Like 'even a dog could do it.'"

Her father Alfonso seized Johan's elbow, anger reddening his cheeks. "She's not your sweetheart." Luigi stiffened, and Johan tugged on his vest while he rocked on his toes. "My eldest daughter, Anya Conti, would like you to be true to your word and teach a woman to operate this boat."

Johan cleared his throat and pointed out the engine key, haphazardly mentioned the accelerator, and then turned his back to the dashboard, nodding at her dismissively. Anya looked over at her father, whose anger seemed dampened slightly by her conspiratorial smile. "So, first I engage this key," she said, smiling a bit to herself as she turned it. The engines fired up, startling Johan and Anya though they both had assumed falsely confident airs. "And before I engage this throttle," she continued, placing her hand carefully and with full knowledge of the challenge she had just issued, "what do I do?"

"You holler to the dock boy to unhook the lines." He said it with fear and uncertainty. "But you're not going to…"

She threw open the window and hollered down to the dock. "Throw off the dock lines." The little dock boy was so shocked to see a woman at the helm that he froze. Johan scurried around the boat encouraging people to either sit or wait on the dock. He hastily closed the engine cover and locked it.

Alfonso leaned forward so that he could be seen through the window. "Throw off the dock lines," he barked, and the little boy sprang into action.

Anya knew she had presented Johan with a dilemma: he couldn't insult family and he didn't want to upset his father, but this was not part of his plan. She gripped the wheel, engaged the engines, and took off in fits and starts, oversteering then correcting as she moved the boat out into the harbor. She and her father exchanged glances: so simple! Straight-backed and in command, she turned the boat and accelerated: the feel of an engine responding in her hands made her smile broadly.

She banked a turn and the passengers stumbled and squealed. Johan stepped in and took back the wheel. "That's enough now; you're frightening people." Alfonso nodded in silent agreement and she relinquished her post.

Johan finished his demonstration, dropped the first load of passengers back at the dock, though Anya wouldn't leave. He took out a second group (with Anya at his elbow), and once the entire harbor was buzzing with news of this new type of vessel, Johan tied the boat at the dock.

"This little beauty is for sale," he called. "See me this weekend to discuss terms."

Johan Hansen was given a hero's welcome by the men of the family, uncles and cousins shaking his shoulders in appreciation and pride. Luigi stood behind him when he sat and patted his blonde hair that was brittle with sea salt. The young women in the family kept their distance and the aunts regarded him dubiously: after all, he was illegitimate. Uncle Luigi's first wife had died 20 years ago, after giving him three short, dark, Italian daughters. The boy had been sired after their mother's death but before his marriage to the Persian, though unsaid was that he was also old enough to be the product of an indiscretion. But he was very respectful to his father's new wife and proper in his manners, which counted for a lot.

In the morning, Johan found Anya on the dock looking the boat over. "I'm sorry for the crack about…dogs," he said nervously. Anya raised her eyebrows but said nothing. "Fact is…I don't know if you've heard of Dorothy Levitt, but she just won the motorboat speed contest. Seriously. In all of France. A woman." Anya looked at him skeptically, but he pulled from his vest pocket an article that had been clipped out and folded. He showed her, then insisted she keep it. "I'll take you out again. Peace offering."

Without another word, Anya stepped into the boat and assumed the helm. She knew Johan hadn't meant that he would take her out immediately, but he threw off the dock lines and saluted her to denote their readiness. This time, Anya pulled away from the dock and headed straight for the opening of the harbor. She had never been beyond it and, when she shot through the arches and out into the Mediterranean, she laughed. To be out on the open water, she thought, no tether, anchor, or plan, she would be freer than even during her childhood meanderings. There was no road, animal track, or signpost. The boat was self-contained, a layer of steel away from disaster, and it demanded her command of it—the only thing that ever had: she was an incompetent assistant to her sister, a clumsy chocolatier, and a begrudgingly obedient daughter. But this! This wildness!

"I want to buy this boat."

Johan chuckled indulgently. "Yes, she's a fun little ride."

"I'm serious. Draw up the papers, cousin. I'm going to buy this boat." Maybe her father would invest in it, or loan her the money.

They wrangled about it until finally Johan put his hands on his hips and came clean.

"Look, truth is, I won the boat in a card game just up the coast and I figured it was worth some money. I brought it into the harbor because…I don't really know anything about boating. Don't tell anyone. I should have said 'so easy even *I* can pilot it.' It wouldn't be right to…sell it to you. But did the sales pitch sound convincing?" He brightened, and Anya was charmed by his childlike excitement over his ploy.

Anya paced the deck. "If you don't sell boats or race boats, what is it that you do?"

"I…" He made indistinct hand gestures as if trying to mold clay. "…seize opportunities." His blue eyes were bright as he gave her a broad, mischievous smile.

***

That night, the entire family sat down at a long table set out in the sand, with votive candles throwing light across the soft linen tablecloth. Johan regaled his father and all sitting near him with stories of his time in the North Sea, a job logging in Russia, an encounter with a pack of wolves, stumbling through a blinding snowstorm into a hunter's lodge where three nuns had sought refuge. He was off again in the morning, Johan announced, and his father was crestfallen but proud that his son had important engagements.

It was very late when the families dispersed, and Alfonso was surprised to see Anya heading away from the beach house and toward the water. The moon was a sliver so the beach was very dark, but Alfonso followed Anya as she trudged through the scrunching pebbles, then the deep sand, then the hard-packed moist sand, where he was finally able to catch up to her and grab her by the shoulders. Anya crumpled onto her knees and he went down with her.

"Please, Papa, please. Help me. I have to go. I have to be somewhere," she pointed out to the ocean.

He scooped her up in his arms and held her close to his chest. She was cursed or blessed with the need to see what was around the bend. His own father had refused to take him on his travels until he was grown, and, as a boy, Alfonso would stand just outside their front door each time his father departed, downcast once again that his father was leaving. But years later when he did travel with his father, he discovered that it wasn't his father's presence he longed for. It was the new vista: no more of the simple house, the gate, the unchanging route out of town, the backside of his father. The hunger had felt like a love for his father but was really a love for the road. From then on, the wanderlust dug inside his chest at night and his belly during the day. It was only Gemma's consistent love that had tamed it. And here was his oldest daughter, clutching the fabric on his shirt, weeping as he had never seen her, more stifled than he had ever been and therefore more passionate about her escape.

"Papa, a transport business. You saw there was enough room for cargo. I have my trousseau money…for the boat…please."

Alfonso kissed her head but was adamant. "It's no life for a woman, Anya."

***

Early in the morning, Alfonso sipped his coffee while he watched Johan stock the boat with fresh water and a tearful Luigi pressed on him supplies of salami, bread, wine, and an odd assortment of things that he thought his son might need. Johan pulled away from the dock, Luigi waving despondently. The death of Alfonso's young sons meant he would never have a moment like this, so uniquely for fathers and sons: bittersweet loss, pride of purpose, vicarious adventure. He stuffed his hand in his coat pocket and was surprised that it was full. He retrieved a letter; it was from Anya. Reading of her intentions to stow away, he dropped his coffee cup in the sand and ran to the dock just as Johan cleared the archway and disappeared into the Mediterranean.

***

Crouching in the cargo hold with a small bag of her belongings, Anya felt her resolve strengthening as the boat rocked beneath her. Despite so many years of playing in the little harbor, being on the Mediterranean surprised her like waking up to a sudden snowfall on a familiar landscape. This boat or another, she would find a way to stay at sea.

She had to stay hidden until they were far enough away from the harbor and her father to make it impractical to turn around and redeliver her. In fact, she hadn't considered what she would do if he simply spun the boat in the opposite direction to take her back. After several hours of fretting while she grew cramped and thirsty, Anya pushed up the cargo hold and stepped onto the deck.

Johan jumped back in shock and then shut down the motors.

"Hear me out, cousin," she said frantically.

Johan blustered around the deck. "You can't be here! Uncle Alfonso…"

"I wrote him a letter and…he was the one who taught me…to sail…and navigate."

"I have to take you back!"

"No, you don't. I have a…business proposition."

Johan spun around as if she might be talking to someone else.

"Transport. Delivering cargo. You said yourself that this boat is more reliable…maneuverable. Regardless of the wind we can deliver. No crew to shovel coal, just lean, and profitable. A partnership, cousin."

***

In the late morning, Johan grew nervous as he watched Anya study the nautical charts that she said she had surreptitiously traded with the innkeeper. He didn't know how to read them and wasn't sure he wanted to learn. When he had won the boat, he had motored away from the dock for fear the loser would try to reclaim it, and, hoping that it drove like a car, he'd hugged the coast until reaching the first harbor, which turned out to be the site of the Conti reunion. He had spun the boat in a tight circle to attract potential buyers, but then realized that he had never docked a boat and could shatter his winnings and even kill himself in the process. Hopefully, his jubilation at a smooth docking would be interpreted as excitement over the product. Pulling back out into the Mediterranean this morning, he was disappointed that he still had the boat, and now Anya was planning a business around it. Unnerved, he motored north toward the next harbor, a potential buyer, and more importantly, a card game with high stakes.

Anya poked her head into every storage unit and cubbyhole, calculating their holding capacity out loud, and over a lunch of bread and cheese, Johan let slip that he supposed he could use a proper profession and transport seemed sensible.

"Women came in handy in negotiations," he said with his mouth full. "They're good distractions." Anya scowled and, to recover, he insisted she describe the profit potential again, the process for the transactions. They nervously discussed sleeping arrangements: she would take the cabin, of course, and he would sleep in a hammock.

They boated north, and since no one could see them, Johan let Anya take the helm while he lounged on the back-bench seat with his feet up on the cargo hold. It was easy going and the sun was warm on their shoulders. At dusk, Johan insisted that he act as captain when they pulled into the next port.

"Stay with the boat," he ordered as he hit the pilings in their slip so hard that the dock shook. He needed a stiff drink, he said. He didn't mention the card game.

***

Late that night, lying in bed but not sleeping, Anya heard fast footfalls on the pier. She threw back the covers when she heard Johan throw off the dock lines and jump into the boat.

He stumbled and fell against the wall of the cabin, clutching his side. "Go!" He waved toward the ocean.

Anya darted to the helm, still in her nightgown. She took them straight out, violently bouncing over the waves, and headed north. She piloted for more than an hour, waiting for Johan to come into the pilot house and explain. But there was no sign of anyone chasing them, and who on earth could catch a motorized boat anyway? Anya shut down the engines, making note of their position relative to lights on the shore so she could ensure that they didn't drift too far. Johan was not on the back-bench, so she called for him in the cabin, then looked around the side of the small pilot house.

Johan lay in a pool of blood, motionless. His formal white shirt and his vest were rent open. Anya fell to her knees, calling out to him. He was unresponsive. Her hands slipped in the blood and she slammed her elbow onto the deck, nearly falling on top of him. The puddle of blood rolled with the motion of the boat. Johan was dead. She sat beside him, put one hand on his chest, covered her eyes with the other, and wept.

It was impossible for her to tell what had happened, and she wasn't going to return to that dangerous town to find out. What would she tell Uncle Luigi? Her father? Worst of all, Johan had died without last rites. She should take him somewhere for a proper Christian burial.

But as she darted around the boat looking for maps, lights, then changing her clothes, she suddenly paused. She knew what it would mean if she took him inland or alerted her family: she would be wrestled back up the mountain again to spend her life grinding hazelnuts and wrapping Easter eggs. She rolled the maps back up.

She got her rosary from the cabin and covered Johan with a sheet though it was soon soaked with blood. She prayed for him. She prayed for herself, now adrift, literally. What had seemed like adventure now felt like a nightmare: she was alone, in the sea, the little 40-foot steel hull boat her only refuge. What on earth made her think she could do this? And how odd that though she was the only one who knew anything about the navigation, she had been more confident with him there. Poor Johan. Killed so young, dying without family to hold him. She prayed and wept.

Several hours later clarity returned, despite the borderless ink-black sea and shapeless jet-black sky around her. She considered her options. Burial at sea could be performed by a ship captain rather than a priest. That was reasonable, wasn't it? On the other hand, how selfish was that, to deny her cousin a proper burial, so she could be free?

She got to her feet with resolve and turned the sheet into a shroud, using a heavy rope to lash him into it. *You understand, don't you cousin? I can't go back.* She shuddered with guilt but proceeded. She weighted the body and, standing at Johan's feet, delivered a hodgepodge of prayers that she hoped sounded like a proper funeral. It was certainly heartfelt. She struggled to raise him over the handrail, staggering with bent knees. But the splash he made when he hit the water and the spectral sight of the white shroud receding into the sea destroyed her resolve, and she slid to the deck and began weeping again.

15

Alfonso had looked like he was dancing in the deep sand toward the receding image of Johan's boat. He pivoted and stepped toward the beach house to confer with Gemma, but realizing that he was not clear about his own attitude to his daughter's flight, he was unprepared for any discussion with his wife. Should he tell his Cousin Luigi? The rest of the family would be scandalized. And what if Johan became heavy-handed and abandoned her at the next harbor? He smiled slightly to himself thinking of his headstrong daughter. Just let him try! On the one hand, he cheered her (a bold move, worthy of a smuggler!) and on the other, he was frightened for her.

The next two hours of his family's packing and departing were a jumble of secrets and conflicting emotions. Before he told Gemma, he gripped her forearm tightly and, looking into her eyes, made her pledge that there would be no scenes in front of his family, no hysteria, and in fact, none of this was the others' business, so she was to act as if all was well. He called Delfina over, held both his wife's and his daughter's hands, and told them the news. When they shrieked, he pulled sharply on their wrists. He was unwilling to share the letter and told them to say their goodbyes to the family without mentioning Anya to anyone. If asked, she was still in the beach house or already on the bus. After hugs and half-truths, Alfonso and his family were on the bus to the train.

Settling the women into a second-class car, Alfonso went into the bar car where no women ventured, and he ordered brandy and a cigar. Was he abandoning Anya, leaving her to her plan with her cousin? It was what she had pleaded for, and he remembered the desperate look of her crouched in the sand begging to be released. If she had been one of his sons (God rest their souls, so small and still, their faces pale and confused on the white sheets) this would have been a scene of joviality, applauding the young man's grit and wily ways. Instead it was something that could barely be spoken. He finished his brandy but stayed in the bar car until just before their arrival.

Alfonso maintained his authority, and his family kept a stiff and silent dignity all the way back to the confectionary, where Delfina and Gemma both rounded on him. She was engaged in a business venture, Alfonso explained. She was in good hands, he insisted weakly, since none of them had known Johan for more than a day. Transport is a family tradition, he said.

Gemma was distraught, bumping into tables and doorjams. She shouted at her husband and wept with sobs that shook her shoulders.

"Let her go," Alfonso brushed his hand over her hair and took her in his arms, but she shrugged him off and looked at him with eyes of knives.

Gemma went into Anya's bedroom and held the blanket that was infused with her daughter's smell of rosemary and vanilla. Once again, Gemma was reduced to clutching fabric that a woman she loved had left behind. She was inconsolable.

***

Gemma would not speak to Alfonso. She rolled over to face the wall every night, set his coffee in front of him in the morning without comment, refused to speak during meals, and soon the atmosphere was so tense that no one spoke at the dinner table at all. Alfonso—who hauled supplies, cut the chocolate from large bricks with the guillotine clever, and staffed the store in front—received all requests from Gemma through Delfina. A cold, silent sadness spread to the confectionary kitchen. Alfonso considered their options in how to answer queries from the villagers, and decided on something approximating the truth: their daughter had taken a job with a transport business out of Rapallo; they were very proud. In the face of Gemma's tight-lipped rage, neighbors chose not to press the issue.

Three weeks into the silence, Alfonso started going down to a disreputable hideaway bar in the back of the laundress's house, where men drank until they fell asleep on the settees and beer-stained chairs. He missed the comfort and companionship of his wife; he missed his beloved daughter, and a part of him longed to be on the water with her. He knew what she was feeling: the thrill just before the ship sails, the extra briskness of the morning when the wagons are ready and the horses are stomping, the excitement after a snow when you're the first one out. He carried her letter in his pocket as a token of her trust in him, as his small connection to the excitement. He had not shown the letter to Gemma, and since he now feared that she would tear it to bits, he had no intention of ever letting her see it. Apparently, the price of his daughter's freedom would come out of the quality of his marriage.

***

Anya started with small operations and arrangements to refuel while she struggled with guilt and fear. She remembered Johan in her morning and evening prayers, lit candles for him in every church in every port she visited but her nightmares were vivid and chastising. Tired and bungling from sleepless nights and inexperience, she shuttled crates of honey from Livorno to Genoa. Olives picked up in Rapallo were delivered to Sanremo. She transported a trio of bleating goats in the middle of a summer storm and, though they were tied to the pitching boat, they fell onto the deck and were dragged around by the swell. Initially, Anya was paid just for her transport services, but sometimes she could scrape together enough money to buy in bulk and sell for a profit. Cases of anchovies in oil could double her money. Barrels of nails returned 40%, and rope, though barely profitable, took her to a seaside town where the pastries were particularly good.

As the months went on, Anya's nightmares became paler and days became imbued with the excitement of escape: the mornings were brighter, sharper, more vivid because she woke in solitude. Every glassy harbor was a personal kindness, every choppy sea an invitation to learn, and every morning that she woke with the boat rocking beneath her, she thanked God that she wasn't relegated to a kitchen in an apron smeared with chocolate. Anya learned to fish off the stern and make small repairs to the motor. Soon she lived barefoot whenever she was offshore, and she bought a pair of loose fitting pants that made her gleefully doubt her own identity.

That September, fearful of the storm season, she docked the boat at Rapallo to return to her mountain village. She entered the confectionary through the front door and wept over the sight of her father as he hurried from behind the counter and threw his arms around her. He cradled her head against his chest and looked up in gratitude to heaven. But when he pulled away she gripped his forearms.

"Papa, I need to tell you…"

Alfonso called to his wife. But before Gemma entered the store from the kitchen, Anya stepped toward her father again, trying to signal that she had bad news to share. "Later," he said under his breath.

***

Unbeknownst to Anya, Gemma assumed that her "adventure" in the transport business was over and that she was home for good. The family threw a party for the entire town, and her sister made a chocolate sculpture of Anya's boat. Delfina strung lanterns between the trees, the children's choir sang, and the candles on the tables twinkled against the chocolate boat like starlight on dark water.

The village women smiled but looked at Anya carefully, trying to detect a hint of ruination that must surely come from freedom. Gemma would have none of it, pulling onto the dance floor any woman who contemplated Anya too long or whispered behind her hand. Her daughter was home and that was all that mattered.

***

Late that night, after a lot of wine, villagers broke pieces off the chocolate boat to eat it, and Alfonso, filled with some of his private grappa, felt it was a bad omen.

When both Gemma and Delfina were on the dance floor, Anya pulled her father aside, and in the alley behind the kitchen, tearfully told him of Johan's fate, and that she had secretly buried him at sea without a priest's intercession.

He held her as she wept, and she told him about the prayers, the candles, the shroud. The guilt. What could he tell Cousin Luigi, he wondered, but the sudden realization that she had been alone all of these months sunk in and he was chilled by the danger of it. It was not safe to be alone on the sea, man or woman, he scolded, and insisted she not reveal this to anyone until he had thought it through.

"Your mother has been very distraught, but it's over now and you're safe, that's all that matters."

"Over? I'm returning to it in the spring, Papa. It's...where I belong."

Alfonso closed his eyes to steel himself.

In the morning, Gemma was tired but chipper when she set the first cup of coffee in front of her daughter.

"We've missed you at the hazelnut station," Gemma said. "My poor old hands just can't do all that grinding. But you're back now."

"Just until the Spring," Anya said firmly.

Gemma railed against her daughter until Delfina closed all the windows so the neighbors wouldn't hear. Anya did her best to explain her plans rationally (though leaving out news of her cousin) but Gemma, in her desperation, began a tirade about fallen women and useless wandering, the cruelty of ungrateful children, the whores and brigands one finds dockside, the pointlessness of life anywhere but here. She forbade Anya to leave, and chased her through the kitchen and the apartment upstairs as Anya hurriedly packed her things. Anya slammed out of the back door and was headed down the hill when

Alfonso caught up with her.

"Stay through the storm season, little one," Alfonso pleaded, though the look on her face made it clear his request was in vain. He rubbed his forehead. "Hug the coast. Take on a crewman. Don't take a dangerous job just for money. I will… send your dowry, your trousseau money so you don't have to go out when the weather is bad." He grabbed her arm. "Please, sweet girl, promise me."

She nodded, choking back tears and started downhill again a little slower.

"Where can I reach you," he called after her. "Where can I write?"

"The Rapallo post office," she said, rushing back to hug him one last time before she left.

It was the last time they would ever see her.

16

Anya had a rough time finding business in the winter. Most cargo transferred to wagons and trains because of the weather. She nursed a timidity when she came into new ports, hiring little boys to fetch groceries rather than marching into town looking for new business. The dearth of work forced her to improve her ability with the backroom negotiations and the bluff, the staged conversation in the alleyway, the boat that starts to pull away but doesn't. She created more cargo space by removing the berth and hanging a hammock as Johan had done. She persevered: she lost money, but she also made a few connections and then a string of good deals. The cartons, flapping their finely written white labels for Conti Transport, produced enough profit to give her a sturdy skirt, a new pair of trousers, touch-up paint, spare parts and dock lines, a new dress for shore, and something for the bank.

That spring, though she was only marginally successful and spent too much time searching for fuel, she crested the waves in the sunshine, her hair loose out behind her as if in triumph. She loved the hundred different sounds that sand and gravel made and how it changed through the night: the surf and its different song when against rock, buoys, or sandy shore. It was a magnificent feeling to be utterly alone, flopped out on the deck of her boat with abandon. She wondered if the boat-racing Dorothy Levitt had ever felt this way, and she unearthed the clipping and tacked it to the wall of the pilot house for inspiration. What woman is ever alone? In the house of one's father then the house of one's husband then the home for one's children: where does a woman ever find solitude? The question made her laugh from her belly as if she had managed to hoodwink the world. She wanted to stop time from passing: with the breeze and the starlight, she had no need for another moment, another wave.

But for every uplifting wave of joy at her freedom, Anya crashed afterward into the trough of loneliness, uncertainty and guilt. Families playing on the grass as she motored past parks showed her what she'd never have. Lovers bankside brought tears to her eyes. Fog and channel marker bells were the sight and sound of her vulnerability.

***

Gemma and Alfonso spent winter and spring in a locked, silent battle. Alfonso was livid that his wife had driven their daughter away, and Gemma was beside herself that Alfonso refused to chase her down. Gemma, who had spent decades in loving communion with her husband and with tenderness toward her children, now seemed to tap into the anger of a little girl who dug for coins in her father's pants while he was passed out. She ordered that Anya's and Johan's names never be spoken in the house, and so she didn't know of Johan's death. Despite that it felt like treachery to not write to him, Cousin Luigi—who never wrote to Alfonso after the reunion anyway—didn't know that Anya had been aboard, and so the family was not considered a source of information about Johan.

At first, Anya sent her father a note with no return address, cryptically telling him that "the poems of Capt. Zedoary can be found at the bottom of the hill," which he interpreted as the post office in the next village. The moment he fetched the letter, he hurriedly wrote back to her, care of the post office in Rapallo, and thereafter, little objects arrived at the post office for him with brief notes and no return address: a beautiful glass jar of olives from Sardinia, a well-aged bottle of Sicilian vinegar. He noted the chronology of their arrival and their places of origin to track her movements.

Alfonso secretly put the foodstuffs on the kitchen shelf where they were incorporated into meals, which made him feel a bit closer to his daughter and as if he was graciously allowing Gemma to share in Anya's gift without challenging her insistence on silence. But as Gemma's wordless and sexless regime continued, it spawned a rancor in Alfonso: he set a bottle of wine and a jar of marinated tomatoes in the middle of the dinner table as if challenging Gemma to ask. Gemma may have wondered but she never did.

Alfonso made a trip down the hill to the other village every two days while Gemma took her afternoon nap. He kept Anya's letters in a box and then sold an old buggy that was stored in a garage next to the confectionary. He locked the doors and kept the windows shuttered, but spent every afternoon naptime there until the walls were festooned with Conti Transport letterhead, all the sketches of beach life that Anya had sent, a map with pins designating her route, and the empty wine bottles and boxes of goodies she had sent.

***

In the early fall, a box addressed to Delfina and wrapped in plain brown paper arrived at the confectionary. The return address said simply "Capt. Zedoary." Alfonso was on edge seeing it on the front counter of the store. Surely Gemma heard his childhood chant with Anya; she had to deduce that this was from their daughter. But Gemma and Delfina cooed over the box and, inhaling deeply, opened it to find cocoa powder. It smelled rich and smooth and the two immediately went into the kitchen. Delfina brought newly made chocolate roses on a special platter; Alfonso set them apart and the three of them, sampling the wares, nodded their heads appreciatively.

When the first customers arrived, Delfina whispered to them. "These are new. Made with chocolate from Capt. Zedoary."

Alfonso heard the young women titter behind their hands and relish the secret of a captain as much as they did the chocolate. The candies were of extremely high quality and when they were gone the richness and depth of the chocolate was transferred to the reputation of Capt. Zedoary and the mystery of Capt. Zedoary added a special allure to the chocolates.

When the second box arrived three weeks later, also with the simple return address of Capt. Zedoary, Gemma and Delfina were more excited.

"Who do you think this is?" Delfina was baffled.

"An admirer." Gemma seemed giddy, Alfonso thought. "Your chocolates are quite renowned, you know."

"Anya…" Alfonso began but Gemma wheeled around on him.

"I said her name was not to be spoken. That Anya would be jealous of this admirer is of no consequence." Gemma turned back to her oldest daughter.

Alfonso threw up his hands.

"The fact is," Gemma continued, "you have someone who apparently cares very much for you, someone who graciously sends you exquisite product, this one postmarked from Sardinia."

Delfina blushed and pursed her lips together as Alfonso had seen her do to suitors in their sitting room.

"He's like you, Alfonso," Gemma said standing between the kitchen and the store front. "Like an admiring spice merchant." And just as Alfonso was about to shout out the truth, the bell on the door jangled and four young women clustered around the platter. "Are these from Capt. Zedoary," they asked breathlessly.

Alfonso could not reveal the source of the chocolate while there were customers in the shop and besides, continuing the secrecy was Gemma's order. And the secret aura was apparently good for business.

But the packages' effect on Delfina was unacceptable to Alfonso. He was his beloved oldest, her mother's daughter. As soon as the post was delivered, Delfina would rush to the storefront, and Alfonso saw the dreamy look in her eyes as if she was hoping for a love letter. "Anything from the captain, father?"

Gemma stood in the hall between kitchen and storefront. "Your secret beau!"

"I will not have this!" Alfonso barked as he slammed his fist on the counter. He was so rarely insistent or demanding that the women froze. "There's no address, no way to find this… Capt. Zedoary and I will not have you wasting your life dreaming about someone who… for all intents and purposes does not exist. Gemma, Delfina is clearly ready for marriage and you are to find someone who is local. And honorable." The surprised women nodded their acquiescence. And while it course-corrected Gemma into a concerted hunt for a son-in-law, Alfonso's prohibition just heightened Capt. Zedoary's appeal to Delfina. He was not just secret fruit, but now forbidden, secret fruit.

It was astounding to Alfonso that Gemma didn't guess the origin of the chocolate packages. She had a daughter in the transport business and packages were being transported. But the siren song of a mysterious lover was too compelling, apparently, and the rarity of the chocolate improved the reputation of the confectionary and the business.

Even as Gemma orchestrated a steady stream of suitors, Delfina had a faraway look, like a jilted woman though she was a virgin, like a wife with a husband at sea, pained by the separation but clutching the warmth of deep love. Alfonso heard her comparing the suitors to the captain and even on her wedding day, Alfonso went into Delfina's room to collect her and found her sitting with a tall stack of the strips of brown paper that contained just the signature of Capt. Zedoary and the postal markings. She had tied them together with ribbon and she smoothed them with her palms. Seeing her father, she jumped up and hid them behind her back.

It broke Alfonso's heart: his wife had banished one daughter and had encouraged the other to live pining for a fabrication.

***

Conti Transport moved small quantities of spices, cheese and chocolate. Merchants cheated her. Thieves broke in while she was at church and emptied her hold. She was overcharged for repairs and sometimes denied dock space outright, but she took comfort in the clink of wine bottles as she bounced over the waves. By now, gas-powered boats were not as unusual and fuel easier to acquire. She rounded the boot of Italy and started trading in the Adriatic, much to her father's consternation, which Anya tried to assuage by sending little sketches of Catholic churches where she would go to mass while on her route. She accompanied each letter with a fine bottle of Croatian wine and artisanal chocolate.

Every year, Alfonso's letters asked her to come home during the storm season, home for Christmas, his birthday. He sent negotiating tips and notice of popular new items that might prove to be an opportunity for her, told her of the popularity of the confections made with the chocolate she had sent, and the growing reputation the shop had for exotic chocolate (though no mention of the legend of the imaginary suitor). Her father's letters made it clear that her mother's opinion hadn't changed but he never spoke of the fury of her mother toward him or the loneliness it caused, and he always closed with a reminder of his pride in her.

Her letters in turn were brief, but she was crestfallen when she was told of Delfina's marriage but had received no invitation and she was bereft with every announcement of Delfina's children. She never asked about her mother or acknowledged the requests to come home.

During that winter's storm season, she bought a large, sturdy boat from an old man who said he couldn't take another winter beating against his ship, while he pressed his ring of keys into Anya's hands as if marrying off his daughter.

She named it *The Zedoary* and supervised the replacement of the steam engine with gas. She improved her inventory techniques, created bills of lading with her name written with a flourish, and was very particular about the accuracy of her work as well as the quality of the chocolate. To grow any larger though, Anya would have to take on crewmen. Though it meant more profit, it would cost her precious solitude so as a stopgap, Anya hired men on docks in all her ports to load and unload her boat. She carried the boxes of chocolate to the post office herself.

That winter was particularly cold and damp, and a rogue wave off the shore of Ancona drenched her as she tried to lash down a box that had broken loose. By the time she pulled into port two hours later, she was feverish and weak.

Luckily, she would think later, she had changed into her dress and was in a store gathering provisions when she collapsed from the flu, not alone at sea or on the dock in her pants, where she might be mistaken for a drunk. As it was, no one would touch her because the outbreak had already taken a number of villagers. Shoppers fled the store and the merchant kept a handkerchief over his mouth and nose while he sent for dockworkers. He let the apples that had tumbled out of her basket skitter across the floor, and the sack of flour that burst as it fell wasn't swept up until she had been taken away. Even the dockworker would not keep her in his home with his children, but put her in a little room in the back of the house of the oldest grandmother in the port and burned the basket Anya had carried.

In her delirium, Anya saw the light squeezing through chinks during the day, the red flames of the fireplace at night, a blue tin cup regularly brought to her lips, and the dark hand that held it. She remembered that her grandmother had died of influenza, so she struggled to break the fever as if it was something that she could conquer with willpower. She tossed in her bed and wiped her sweat on the threadbare sheets. She ate the bowls of soup they brought her though she wasn't hungry, tried unsuccessfully every day to get out of bed, pushed herself to sit up until the grandmother slapped her shoulder and tucked her in as tightly as a swaddled baby. Falling in and out of the fever, she was overcome by her own loneliness: she saw her parents holding hands...she was running through a forest desperate to return to a place she couldn't name or reach...fish struggled for their life on the line behind the boat...Johan and his shroud descended into the depths...her hands pressed the bow praying that a patch too small for a hole would hold...her father stood on the top of the hill, waiting for her, then growing stooped and flying away as ash...salt spray, like lace, undulated on either side of her...

***

They said that it took two weeks before she finally came out of the

131

fever. When the grandmother returned to the shack with broth, Anya was washing her face in a basin, dressed in an old blue nightgown that wasn't hers. The flu had made her weak and she looked rough.

Her nightmares had convinced her that, sadly, the price of her freedom was isolation, a loveless life with no future, no lineage. No mother's love. No camaraderie with her sister. Comfort from her father delivered in the mail. She was hardly even a woman, she thought—a virgin in trousers alone on a boat.

She saw the women in town with their large, plumed hats and ankle-length dresses standing on the edges of the games or negotiations, never in the center, and while Anya had felt superior, now she hid from their potentially disapproving eyes. Or was she just a coward, afraid to stand up for herself as a different kind of woman and tolerate the look in their eyes? She didn't even have friends, so she didn't know the sticky business of being both accommodating and oneself at the same time. Was there a way to be free but not alone? Apparently not.

As soon as she reached that conclusion, though, she knew she was lying. Anya was an adult: they couldn't imprison her if she returned home for Christmas. She had self-righteously thought her mother was the culprit, putting convention before love, but what was Anya doing? Withholding love to punish her mother? Hurting her supportive father and blameless sister in the process? Even if she didn't speak to her mother, didn't she want to meet her nieces? And was romantic love the only kind? Was family the only company?

***

Anya threw herself into her work and, begrudgingly, took on two young women as deckhands. She bought a boat to ply the Veneto River that she christened *The Galangal* and hired the son of her nursemaid grandmother to captain it. Despite her growing—though still modest—prosperity, she never took a house in any of her favorite port towns or her mountain village, no matter how much her father pleaded. Five years later, she looked ten years older, and her hair was coarser from the wind and salt, her lips deeper lined.

When World War I broke out, Alfonso lost contact with Anya, and

Capt. Zedoary stopped sending packages. The government called upon Anya to shuttle wounded soldiers from the mouth of the Isonzo River to safety in Trieste, a dangerous assignment. She and her deckhands painted all parts of the boat black. She had the boat bottom scraped and all superfluous gear removed, including the trunks of her deckhands, until there was just a stove and nine hammocks—anything to increase speed and decrease noise. She stocked medical supplies and a nurse joined her crew. They devised a nearly silent departure, though it was slower than she would've liked, and more than once, despite the speed at which she drove when out of sight, soldiers died before reaching shore. She grieved every time, cutting a small cross into the doorframe for each man she couldn't save: she made more than 40 trips and cut 14 crosses, plus an extra for Johan.

Battles in the area killed half of all the Italian soldiers who fought in the war. The crew's efforts repelled the German forces mere miles, and then more of her journeys brought the dead than the wounded. In the Asiago Offensive in May 1916, the Germans captured her boat and summarily executed all aboard.

***

When they first received the news, though it was without embellishment or explanation, Gemma cried with bitterness. Alfonso was despondent, as if he had cowardly stayed home while romanticizing the vagabond life that had killed her.

Eight months after the end of the war, a short government official, further dwarfed by the metals pinned to his chest and the lurching way he walked, climbed up the hill to the confectionary. Yards behind him, panting from the effort, struggled two soldiers with one leg each, and another whose face was gnarled with scar tissue. They owed their life to Anya, they said. The official stepped forward and with a curt bow presented Alfonso and Gemma with a bronze plaque honoring Anya's contribution in the war. Crying quietly, Alfonso insisted that they stay for dinner and pressed them for stories of the wartime events. The next morning, the official left, proud that the presentation had gone without a hitch; the soldiers left sad and shaken by the retelling. Anya's parents mounted the plaque on the cement wall beside the confectionary and, breaking years of distance, they held each other and wept.

Three months later, six women with bright blue ribbons on their lapels chattered among themselves as they climbed the hill and, speaking a language no one in the village understood, presented Alfonso and Gemma with a plaque, inscribed in a language no one could read. With hand gestures signifying books, they described a small port school in Croatia that Anya had funded and stocked.

Alfonso greeted them with surprise and joy. After settling them in with his private grappa, he ran to his box of correspondence, unearthed the letter that told of their adventure, and, bringing the letter to the fore, asked them what had happened to Michelle the Tunisian boatman. "What about the preacher?" he asked, and expressed regrets when he learned, through gestures and glum faces, that he had passed.

Gemma now had a new source of resentment: Alfonso had been privy to their daughter's life all this time. When Gemma confronted him with it he held out his hands.

"How can I tell you about someone whose name can't be spoken?"

On the one hand, he was glad to finally have a chance to charge her with this crime, and on the other hand, he felt her pain over having been excluded.

***

Gemma listened to the stories, asked for details and descriptions but her pride would not let her admit the extent of her mistake or ask Alfonso to take her through all the letters, and as a result, she was surprised anew when the next group of people sat down to tell of Anya's heroics: Moroccan descendants of the grandmother who had nursed Anya when she was ill. They thanked Alfonso and Gemma for Conti Transport, recounting riverboat adventures with Anya.

When the Moroccans arrived, Alfonso set up chairs in the alley behind the confectionary. He opened the doors of his secret room to the devotees, his daughter, and the village at large. Delfina stood by her mother's side, then slowly crossed the threshold to see her sister's progression around the Mediterranean and Adriatic. She stopped at a sketch of *The Zedoary*, and as the truth set in, she covered her mouth with her hands. Her husband stepped next to her and she took his arm, resting her head on his shoulder in shame and sorrow.

At first, Gemma was loath to go in. Then, timidly entering a lair she hadn't known existed, she understood how much of life her pride had denied her, how much her strictures on life had cost her. The Moroccans presented a tin vase inscribed with Anya's name that Alfonso mounted on the wall between the plaques.

As groups continued to arrive, the villagers gathered outside Alfonso's room, leaning over each other's shoulders to hear the stories. Dignitaries from orphanages, seaside hospitals, and village water-well projects climbed the hill, recounting tales of medicine delivered just in time, roofing that Anya had brought through a storm to save a church, children's coats delivered every winter, a pump that had revived a crop brought by a captain who would accept no payment. Gemma sat in a straight-backed chair with her hands in her lap as she listened to the grateful guests. They had loved Anya, been loved by Anya. These strangers knew Anya better than her own mother. All this love and kindness had been experienced elsewhere, by others, and now was gone.

Until she died, Gemma ran her hands over each of the plaques every morning on the way to work and every evening on the way home, as if they brought her a little closer to her daughter's life and might serve as a penance. She filled the vase with flowers every week. Before they were destroyed in the Second World War, the wall of plaques meant something to others as well: it became a place where young men leaned on a hand and prayed for bravery; old women begged for intervention; and young women, seeking both love and freedom, hoped to not have to settle for just one.

17

1630

The little village on the top of the hill had been pivotal in the development of the art of chocolate since the cocoa bean's first arrival in Italy in the 1500's. And though it had always been tied up with love, betrayal, and seduction, chocolate had been a closely guarded secret in Spain until then. Not that they knew what they had when they first saw it: Christopher Columbus had brought cocoa beans to the Spanish court, but after rolling them around in her gloved palm, Queen Isabella tossed the beans to the floor, to be crushed by the soft slippers of ladies on their way out of the throne room.

Cortez, on the other hand, knew the power of what he had in his cup when the Mesoamericans had served him the hot, bitter, and strong xocolatl—which was made with chilies and water, not milk. He planted cacao trees in the Caribbean islands before he returned to Europe, and he served the drink to the court, mixing it with the new discovery that was rocking Europe (but was yet unknown to the Mesoamericans)—sugar. For 80 years, it was a drink that was served only to the Spanish nobility, unknown to the other monarchs of Europe, so obscure that pirates capturing a ship filled with it assumed it was useless ballast and set the vessel on fire. But Spain opened its first cocoa processing plant in 1585 and who spreads the word better than people trying to make money? The monks who processed the beans whispered of its deliciousness to French monks, and the mendicants among them spread the word. By the time it reached Italy, the third country to enjoy it, this astounding new substance was considered a powerful aphrodisiac for women, in part because of the amorous exploits of the Duke of Savoy.

Duke Charles Emmanuelle of Savoy, born a short hunchback in 1562, was well-educated, intelligent, and fluent in Italian, French, Spanish, and Latin, but he was nicknamed *"Testa d'feu"*—the hot-headed—some say because of his military aggression, others because of his seemingly insatiable libido. He married Catherine Michelle of Spain, daughter of Philip II and Elizabeth of Valois, and his new wife brought chocolate with her to her new home in Turin, Italy.

And with the chocolate came the chocolatier, a young man whose sole task was the preparation of the drink.

It didn't take the Duke of Savoy long to make the connection between his wife's love of chocolate and her willingness to receive him, nor for the duke to decide that the collaboration of the young chocolatier was essential to his amorous success. He had the Spanish chocolatier train an Italian, then dismissed the Spaniard and elevated the Italian chocolatier—a 15-year-old boy named Amadeo who was even shorter than the duke—to a key position in his retinue.

Amadeo was dressed like a footman, though with a special ribbon denoting his status as key to the bedchamber. He lived in fine rooms on the same level of the house as the duke and traveled everywhere with the couple. The duke had his workmen create a special cart for Amadeo's chocolate supplies so that on a moment's notice, Amadeo could rush to the duchess's bedchamber and prepare the drink just the way she liked it. Facing the wall to avoid staring at the lovers, who were perhaps in bed, perhaps half-dressed, he would set the cup on the edge of the cart for the duke to serve, then was ordered to wait until the Duchess of Savoy's satisfied murmurs over the chocolate turned into hungry murmurs for her husband.

After the birth of their first son, Filippo Emanuele, in 1586, the duke doubled down on his devotion to the chocolate and decreed that Amadeo be given access to any herb, spice, or liqueur—even if they had to be brought by camel or Chinese junk. Especially because of his hunchback, the duke was convinced that the jet-black brew was the sole reason for his sexual success, and Amadeo stood facing the wall of the bedchamber at the conception of their second son, Vittorio, born in 1587. Now the aroma of chocolate became the signal for sex, and whenever it wafted through the palace, women—from the ladies-in-waiting to the baker's lass—took it as permission for love.

Amadeo kept a careful record of the ingredients of each cup: a cinnamon stick for the conception of the heir; a raspberry infusion for the conception of Vittorio; candied orange paste for the conception of Emanuele Filiberto, born in 1588; star anise for Margarita, born in 1589. When the supply of cinnamon dried up in 1590 (border skirmishes followed by a great sandstorm), the duke considered marshaling his forces to break up the battle, but luckily, Amadeo was able to invent a new brew involving ambergris, and Isabella was born in 1591. Vanilla infusions brought them Maurizio in 1593; jasmine flowers, Maria Apollonia in 1594; musk, Francesca Caterina in 1593 and Tommaso Francesco in 1596. Amber in the chocolate conceived the tenth and final child between the duke and duchess, Giovanna, who was born and died with her mother in 1597. (Cosimo de'Medici, the infamous Italian banker during the Italian Renaissance, would later insist that his chocolate drink include all of the above ingredients).

***

Amadeo, now a 28-year-old man, was heartbroken over the death of the duchess and, assuming that he was no longer necessary, was packing his strongbox when the duke brusquely knocked on his door and burst in. There was a beautiful young courtier, the Marchesa

Marguerite de Rossillon, who must be bedded, the duke said. Find the chocolate aphrodisiac for her, Amadeo was ordered. Soon the cart was being wheeled down a different corridor and the aroma of chocolate (with extra sugar and ground, candied apricots) filled the living chambers of the castle once again.

Two months later, during a particularly beautiful spring festival, the courtier Luisa de During Marechal, in a diaphanous dress with fresh flowers in her hair, caught the duke's eye. Now Amadeo had a problem. His chocolate cart could not roll down the hallway for Marguerite de Rossillon one night and then a different hallway for Luisa de During Marechal (honey, extra cocoa) the next, especially since Luisa had conceived and bore the duke a son, whom she named Emanuele, in 1600. The wheels were taken off the cart and footmen ordered to carry it, quietly.

At the summer solstice, though, another mistress, Virginia Pallavicino (vanilla bean and rose) conceived the duke's son Carlo Umberto, and the duke's first mistress, the marchesa, went on a tirade: the aroma of chocolate should come only from her bedchamber, or the duke's, only when Marguerite was there.

The duke had other ideas. The only way to get to all three of his mistresses, undetected, was through the hidden passageways behind the walls so the cart was further reduced to a wooden box almost too large for Amadeo to carry. Velvet-lined, it carried his jar of cocoa powder, bottles and pouches of spices, mortar and pestle for grinding ingredients, tweezers, measuring spoons, a small knife. He wore a thick roll of cloth around his waist and used it to block the aroma from seeping under the door when he mixed his concoctions. Furthermore, his record of the chocolate drinks he served was also a chronicling of the Duke of Savoy's indiscretions, and it became almost more valuable to the duke than the chocolate itself.

When Marguerite gave birth to a son, Maurizio, Amadeo's diary would record a liaison with a fourth mistress, the stunning Argentina Provana (dark, extra chili), and ultimately, the birth of her son Felice. The diary would have alerted Argentina to the first seduction of mistress number five, Anna Felizita Cusani (hazelnut paste), and the conception by mistress one, Marguerite, of her only daughter Margherita. The conception of Silvio by Virginia, mistress three, would coincide with the birth of Ludovico by Anna, mistress four. The marchesa, incensed by the competition, was less willing to entertain the duke, who in turn pressured Amadeo to find another recipe. The addition of nutmeg fostered the conception of Gabriele and distracted her from the birth of Virginia's Vitichindo, the nineteenth child born of the duke.

***

Amadeo was exhausted from the late nights, but knew he was a lucky man. Not only did the most beautiful women in the region respond to his chocolate and reward him with a surreptitious view of exquisite breasts, shapely legs, and perfect feet as they moved under the gold threaded sheets; not only did he spend his evenings surrounded by the sound of sex and the aroma of chocolate, but word got out that he held the key to women's lust so he was secretly asked to parties, invited to join women for slow walks through the garden, included in the picnic at the hunt. The duke made it clear early in Amadeo's employment, though, that the chocolate should not be given to anyone under any circumstances, nor should Amadeo describe his recipes or procedures, and the Testa d'feu, hot-headed duke, was not to be crossed. This gave Amadeo a mysterious air, a man whose counsel was frequently sought but rarely given, a man who had what everyone wanted, both men and women: the ability to make women swoon. His bed was rarely empty, as the lesser courtier women hoped to suck the chocolate from under his fingernails and lick the dust of it off his neck.

Amadeo's idyllic, lascivious life took an unexpected turn, though, with the arrival at court of Sophia Meraviglia, a woman as tall and shapely as the duke was short and misshapen. Her red hair, which she wore up in intricate shapes festooned with silk butterflies and real fruit, made her stand out in any crowd, and at the Easter celebration, the Duke of Savoy took notice. So did Amadeo. Unlike the other court women who clustered around the duke, chittering and fawning, Sophia knelt on the grass with the children, showing them eggs and nearby branches, laughing with them. Her dress was pastel, still fine but simpler in its design, with lace covering the bodice. Amadeo watched her kindness, her modesty, the appreciative way she spoke to the governess and the older children. Standing away from the crowd, he followed her as she moved to the side garden, and just as he was about to step off the path and introduce himself to her, the duke grasped him by the shoulder and, standing behind him, spoke quietly.

"I see you have found her. Doing your research already? Good. Find the chocolate for her by tomorrow." The duke tapped him on the shoulder and walked off, but Amadeo could not move.

This woman was different. For the first time, Amadeo felt conflicted over his task. He very much wanted her to taste his concoctions (the taste of the New World, the results of his hard work and mastery!), but not for the duke's purposes.

Amadeo had realized quickly after joining the duke's staff that chocolate was just a beverage, possessing no magical powers, but at first, it was employment. Then it had been a puzzle to see how many different beverages he could devise with this interesting substance. It was as much a study in new spices as it was in chocolate. Later, Amadeo had reached the age when sex held men in its grip, blinded to other topics, and he was willing to carry on a fantasy in its pursuit. Watching Sophia stroll through the gardens, the sun glinting off her mass of red hair, the breeze making the silk butterflies flutter as if trying to carry her off, Amadeo wanted her. Not just for himself, but to protect her from the Duke of Savoy, to keep her from joining the gaggle of battling mistresses.

That night he made excuses to the duke: he hadn't been successful in finding what she craved; she was a tricky one, he said nervously, hard to figure out. Could he wait another day? The duke scowled but relented. The following day, Amadeo was expected to stay close to Sophia, and he deciphered immediately what she would like (cardamom and honey) but kept it to himself.

The following day's delivery of cocoa beans gave Amadeo another way out. He needed to make sure the cocoa powder was the freshest imaginable, Amadeo improvised in his explanation to the duke, and it would take several days of grinding before the beans were ready. In the meantime, he encouraged the duke to maintain a distance from Sophia, to enhance the surprise and the power of the chocolate. The duke begrudgingly stayed clear of her. The next day Amadeo was seen talking to her in the garden, and when challenged by the duke, explained that he was simply trying to decipher her favorite tastes based on the stories she told. In truth, as a newcomer to the court, she was ignorant of the duke's use of chocolate, and so when courtiers raised their eyebrows over the sight of Amadeo and a woman speaking in the garden, a sure sign that she was the next to be in the duke's bed, she likely thought nothing of it and enjoyed easy flowing conversation with Amadeo in which they described the best flowers and vegetables of their home regions, their favorite cakes, times of year, the deaths of parents and siblings, preference in horses, gardens, and children. He thought she was splendid. He wanted her for himself.

That evening, Amadeo stopped at the duke's study and, while afraid that his nervousness would reveal his ulterior motive, he told the duke of some progress in deciphering the elements for her chocolate, but encouraged him to introduce it slowly, during a casual meeting, not just in the bedchamber. She was a modest and honorable woman, Amadeo explained; she would need his potion for her to become interested enough to even approach the bedchamber. They had never held off before, but the duke agreed. They would meet her in the duke's library tomorrow after vespers.

In the morning, however, Amadeo was startled by banging on his door. When he opened it, still in his bed shirt with his face half lathered for a shave, two footmen grabbed him by the arms and hustled him unceremoniously into the chambers of mistress number one, the Marchesa Marguerite de Rossillon. Her ladies in waiting giggled behind their hands over his spindly, hairy legs, and some of his shaving lather plopped to the floor when he bowed to her. Pacing in front of him, she accused him of treachery, reminded him of her powerful friends, and railed over the bevy of women, all fueled by his chocolate aphrodisiac and bent on usurping her. She was certain she had smelled chocolate just the other night. She knew the signs, and they were now pointing to this new, red-haired beauty, Sophia. Amadeo had to help the her, she commanded: there had to be a way to keep Sophia from the duke's bed.

Amadeo breathed a sigh of relief: in this they were allied. Marguerite ordered a servant to give him a cloth to remove the lather on his face before he further messed up the floor; one of her ladies brought him a sheet to cover his legs. Change the chocolate, she ordered. Make it do the opposite; make it an anti-aphrodisiac. Amadeo knew this was unlikely. She threatened to banish him, and just when she started hinting at more harsh punishments that involved the loss of body parts, he hit upon an idea. Wrapping the sheet around him so that his arms were free, he described an alternate plan.

"Women are...enchanted...by the chocolate because they've never tasted it," he began. "It elevates them to a higher level of...love because it's something they haven't experienced before." If the marchesa were to host a party, for example, where *all* the women drank chocolate, there would be no room for elevation. Nothing kills romance like the ordinary. The ladies-in-waiting clustered around the marchesa: this party would finally let them taste the renowned brew. He thought of Sophia: here was a way she could drink his sublime creation but stay away from the duke. Amadeo warmed to his subject. This would also protect the marchesa in the future, he added, if she served chocolate to every woman who crossed the Duke of Savoy's path.

Marguerite and all the ladies-in-waiting seized upon his idea, and when he mentioned the impending meeting between Sophia and the duke in the library, the party planning began in earnest. "Do it quietly," Amadeo admonished them. "The duke is not to know." The marchesa ordered that the kitchen give Amadeo whatever he needed. They invited all the duke's lovers, every woman in the castle, and all attractive women in the neighboring gentry. Riders were sent out with invitations. Bakers were summoned and cakes commanded. A dozen baths were drawn, hairdressers worked double time, the gardener brought vast quantities of flowers into the library.

Luckily for Amadeo, the duke was surveying back pastureland for the afternoon, which gave Amadeo time to gather the mountain of chocolate powder, sugar, and spices needed for the party, and most importantly, to think of a way to escape the fury of the duke. He ran to his rooms and threw on some clothes, then hurried to the library. He couldn't make individual cups for the individual mistresses: it would be too time-consuming and reveal how complex the aphrodisiacs had become. He had footmen move tables, and the kitchen bring stacks, of cups and after frantically looking through the storerooms; he had them haul in three massive samovar-like urns. One would hold chocolate with chilies as homage to the original Mesoamericans. The middle would include apricot oil, the marchesa's favorite, and the third would contain chocolate without spices in the hopes of inuring the general female public from its power.

When Sophia arrived in the library, early in the hopes she could find a book to borrow, she brightened at the sight of Marguerite. The marchesa, noting that Sophia was unadorned and so perhaps ignorant of the duke's designs, brightened at the sight of her. As the marchesa herself poured Sophia a cup of chocolate, Sophia inhaled deeply and was stunned by an aroma she had never encountered. After the first sip, Sophia looked around the room: steaming cups of an incredible brew, beautiful women in service to one another. By women, about women.

***

Amadeo was not present when the duke arrived to see all his lovers and his pending conquest together in the library, already sipping his secret brew. History does record that he sired just one more child—his 21st—and that he married his first mistress Marguerite in 1629, the year before he died, legitimizing her children though they would not be given succession rights.

Amadeo's interest in Sophia had been extinguished by his sense of self-preservation. He had hastily thrown a few pieces of clothing into a bag in which he had hidden his box of chocolate supplies and fled on any horse the stable would give him. He was never heard from again; some say he rode due south, across the plains, and then straight uphill to an unnamed village that centuries later would have a reputation for outstanding chocolate.

18

Present

Centuries later, in that same village, Luca straightened his tie while holding a bouquet of flowers and a box of chocolates between his knees. He took them up again in his fist, but after climbing just two of the wide stairs up to the village center, shoved them back between his knees, removed his tie, and unbuttoned the collar of his shirt. Maybe he should look casual, though he was wearing his best sports jacket. His toes tapped nervously inside his best shoes.

It wouldn't do to reveal the fact that he had been thinking of Gretchen since he had watched her trudge up the steps on her first day here, that the thought of her made him shave closer, send his clothing to the dry cleaner, get a pedicure just before the salon closed so no one would see a man there. He had obsessively groomed his fingernails, tried to soften away a bit of the calluses on his hands. He hadn't felt this way in a long time, and he alternated between being happy about it as proof that he was still alive, still a man with a little juice left, and irritation that she had put him in this position, vulnerable again after all these years. He had never married, had blown his one shot at it when he had gotten drunk at a friend's bachelor party and woken up in a whorehouse. His devout girlfriend had refused to see him, married someone else shortly afterward, moved away, and now was a fat (and presumably happy) grandmother. Ever since then, he had been the extra guy at the party and the last one invited to the picnic; as he grew older, his social circle was increasingly men-only—three overweight guys watching soccer in the back of a bar at the bottom of the hill. It wasn't a bad life, and whenever he felt poorly about it, some married man would slide into the booth with them and cry in his beer over the damn sexless shame of marriage. Now in his 40's, Luca had accepted his path, after having spent the better part of his 30's grinding away on disappointment and anger.

This renewed interest was surprising, exhilarating, but he felt like a powerful engine that hadn't been turned over in years, sputtering and clanking, hoping for a hearty roar. There was something about Gretchen that made it worth the effort, he thought as he trudged up hill, sweating and worrying about his sweating. Something told him that he could do something about her sorrow. He wanted to be the shoulder she leaned on; something about her drove him here in a polished car and pressed clothes while holding flowers, though she hadn't spoken to him since their original transaction. If he couldn't find her, he reasoned, he could always take the flowers to church or the cemetery behind it. Calmed a bit by knowing he could back out of his plan, he saw the hotelier's youngest son approaching.

"Marco, come here." He beckoned sharply and thrust the box of chocolates into the little boy's chest. "Give these to the American. And not a word of where they're from." He immediately regretted his imposition of anonymity: how did that advance his cause? But it was done now, and all he could do was tuck his shirt deeper into his sweaty waistline and wave the boy off. Luca paced to the alcove created by the altar to the Virgin Mary, put the flowers in a dusty vase. He was just rusty, that was all. His next step would be smoother.

The child looked perplexed by his chore, though Luca could see that he was striding obediently toward the hotel where the American was staying. They called him *Signor Pezzo di Carbone*, Mr. Lump of Coal, Luca knew, either because he was short, dark-haired, and hairy, or because he usually sat in his car for hire. Why Mr. Lump of Coal was sending a package to the American was beyond Marco probably, but when the child saw her sitting on a shaded bench across from her hotel, he thrust the box into her hands and turned to run off. Luca watched from afar, bracing himself for her reaction.

***

Gretchen had returned to her hotel and showered in the hopes that it would snap her back to reality. Dario was very good-looking, but that kiss had jeopardized the life of a man whose status and reputation were in flux, in a small town where reputation mattered. The kiss had been glorious though, even after the searing pain of seeing the children.

She was running her hands through her newly-washed hair, while taking in the last of the sun, both weary and confused, when the child arrived. She incredulously asked about its origins, and he threw up his hands and said something in Italian. Gretchen struggled to get her iPhone out of her pocket and launch the translation app as the child ran off. She tried to repeat his answer into the translation app, but when it returned the answer "lump of coal," she assumed that she had repeated it incorrectly and put the phone away in frustration. Her confusion was heightened when she opened the box and saw chocolates. Was someone mocking her for her inability to produce chocolates this fine? Were these product suggestions? In her fragile state, still reeling from her encounter with the children and the glory of Dario, the box filled her with sadness and a feeling of inadequacy.

She was startled when she looked up from the chocolates and Luca was standing where the child had been.

"Signora." He bowed slightly as they locked eyes. "Come for a drive." He looked down at the box of chocolates in her hands and smiled.

Gretchen was flustered over her sudden understanding that the chocolates were from Luca and that this was not a ride-for-hire, but an excursion, perhaps even a romantic gesture. She thought of Dario, regretting her indiscretion. This was just a little drive though, she reasoned, and she followed Luca to his car.

They drove up winding roads with the tires squealing on the turns, the vistas opening in front of her. They drove through an olive grove and she kept her face as close to the open window as she could without being outside, inhaling the beautiful smell of grass and trees, sunshine on old wooden fences. She smelled basil. She felt disembodied, a wonderful feeling after months of wishing that she didn't exist. Now if she could just get her mind to go numb and be just this feeling—this warmth from sunlight on skin, the rush of a breeze that was a kind of safety, the car's implicit permission to flee.

They drove for nearly an hour while Gretchen asked questions about the landscape, sometimes consulting her phone for the Italian wording. Neither of them asked personal questions and Gretchen found that relaxing, but as they arrived at the village the pain washed over her again, and she insisted that he drop her off at the base of the hill, claiming that she wanted to enjoy the greengrocer's garden.

Luca turned off the engine and watched her walk up the hill. Was her step a little lighter? That would be a good sign. Was it faster than usual? That would be a bad one. *Nicely done*, he complimented himself. It had gone well. Every time she had exclaimed on their drive, Luca had smiled broader and relaxed a little more. He knew that her brightness was being created by the vistas, not by him, but it had been his idea and he hoped that she made the connection. And the thought of all the years that he had spent without someone exclaiming over the vista, without a woman to pamper, tried to encroach on his good mood the way a sip of water reminds you how thirsty you have been. *No*, he thought, *this time would be different*.

***

Dario sat at the head of the long table in the courtyard behind his restaurant with the envelope of divorce papers rolled up in his hand and his head hung. He hadn't showered last night, just sat in a chair in a stupor, and now his armpits and neck were sticky. He hadn't shaved this morning: what was the point? But there was a roast to be basted; he'd seen Paolo poke his head into the courtyard a couple of times, scowl at him, then open the oven door himself. How could this have come to divorce? Dario didn't know if his incredulity made him seem like more of a victim or more of a bad husband: he had had no idea that she was unhappy enough to leave him.

On the other hand, his reaction to the American weeping in his arms had surprised him as well. She was beautiful and wounded. She had needed him, treated his embrace as solace, not just an easily-ignored, everyday action. Her hair had smelled delicious, and though he didn't remember exactly what his wife's smelled like, it didn't smell like hers and that alone was exciting. So here he was, nearly as guilty as his wife.

Looking down at the divorce papers, he had to acknowledge that he thought there was a chance at reconciliation, that if he could just summon the strength to forgive her all would be well; he had dawdled finding that forgiveness. No one in the family knew how to get in touch with Rosa, but he hadn't tried very hard. He had wallowed in his position as the jilted husband. He wouldn't say that life wasn't worth living without her, but it seemed much paler now. He took off his apron and threw it on top of the divorce papers.

He stood outside the kitchen, his hands gripping the doorframe. "You've got this, don't you, Paolo? I'm going to…" and he motioned behind the restaurant.

"Papa, you're on the grill tonight!" Saturday, all hands on deck.

Dario shook his head. "You'll be fine."

"You can't just—" Paolo stepped away from the stove, wiping his hands on his apron, calling to his father. Dario, on the far side of the courtyard, turned as Paolo lurched back to the stove, gave a pan heaped high with onions a shake, and returned to the door. Dario threw up his hands. Paolo shook his head and went back to the stove.

Dario walked to a bench that was perched on the hill overlooking the valley, just where the road started its steep downward slope at the edge of the village. The wind swooping uphill buffeted his face as if denying him permission to move. Dario sat with his forearms on his knees until after the lunch rush hour, then went home and slept the rest of the afternoon.

Sunday morning, he sat in a chair in his bedroom until Paolo gave up pounding on the door and went to the restaurant alone. Then Dario rose and, without shaving, walked to the end of the village to resume his spot on the bench. He walked downhill toward the church but couldn't bring himself to go in, and he got a cup of black coffee and an orange at the low-end bistro, as if he was divorcing himself from cuisine. The following day, he walked the perimeter of the village starting at the bench and proceeding north to south, then pivoting when he reached the bench and returning south to north. He wore sunglasses, then added a hat that obscured most of his face—though no one who walked by him, even the children who took it upon themselves to creep up behind him when he was on the bench, had heard him cry.

***

That first night that his father had abdicated his position as chef, Paolo was furious. Late that night, he went home in a white heat, but he couldn't rouse Dario from his room no matter how incendiary his accusations, nor could he get a response from his father the following morning. Paolo checked for him in the small room between the restaurant and kitchen that had always held a daybed (so, when children, Adelina and Paolo could take their naps, do their homework, and stay out from under foot). When they became adults, his father began using it for a mid-afternoon nap between seatings. No sign of him there, either.

When it was clear that they were about to run out of supplies, Paolo begrudgingly ordered from the butcher, the greengrocer, and the vintner. But as they were one person short, there was no fresh pasta, no carefully-tended risotto, and the food was mismatched.

The third day, Paolo rapped sharply on his father's door and, having seen evidence of his father's return though not his father, he trudged off to the restaurant before sunrise. He surprised himself that within two blocks he was thinking solely of the menu rather than his father's absence. That day, he produced the entirety of the menu without fail, but many of the dishes were either too heavy for the weather, missing an ingredient that Paolo had overlooked in his shopping list, or not delivered *en masse* to the table. Patrons started to grumble, and Paolo knew that his mistakes were just adding to the scandal of his mother's departure.

Still, the new position as chef was exciting, and between meals he had enough energy to place another order for ingredients for new entrées—his entrées.

19

Adelina stepped into her mother's role as hostess and waitress, thankfully the busboy stayed, and the kitchen helper was happy to be temporarily promoted to sous chef. Adelina did her best to charm the patrons to make them forget her brother's mistakes. She knew she was a good waitress, having watched her mother throughout her childhood while sitting on a barstool with crayons or her homework, fortified by steamed milk with almond. Now, people were so pleased to see her that it was difficult to remember her worry that returning would be construed as failure. And their bright and joyous welcomes didn't reveal any indication that her return was part of the family scandal. They chuckled at her witty greetings. As she set down small plates of beet salad the second evening of her father's absence, feeling the fabric of her skirt brush against her warm bare legs, she had to acknowledge that the restaurant patrons made her feel beautiful. They made her feel precious.

But the thing that was precious to her now was the chocolate. In the restaurant, a cut of meat would start out bloody, marbled with fat, flopped on the fire for a violent searing, or endure a tortuously long roast, then be attacked with the cleaver. Looking around at the blocks and pastilles of chocolate, it seemed to her that chocolate was beautiful when it started. It cooked beautifully, and it ended as something exquisite. There was a gentleness there.

Returning home after helping Signora Liguria, she'd downloaded to her tablet several books on working with chocolate and spent most of the night reading on techniques. She had dreamt about chocolate. She imagined herself behind the long work table and it calmed her at the same time that it was exciting. Painting had never made her feel this way. Was there a confectionary school nearby? Was this something she could get a degree in? Could she apprentice to Signora Liguria? Would she go back to Rome? No, she immediately told herself. Not to Rome. The old woman was the key.

The next morning, after another sleepless night of studying, Adelina set out toward the confectionary shop with a plan in mind. She arrived just as Signora Liguria was opening the side door.

"Excuse me, Signora Liguria. I was wondering if you agree with this procedure for making white chocolate." She showed her the section in the tablet.

Signora Liguria was taken aback. "Why do you want to know?"

"You were so wonderful to let me help you with the chocolate…" She was laying it on a little thick, she knew. "I'm completely bewitched." That much was true, but now came her tactic. "I'm thinking of making it my profession. Opening a little shop."

"In this village? You will do no such thing! *I* am the village chocolatier." Signora Liguria pushed open the door with her cane and strode angrily toward the kitchen. Her hair was pinned extra tightly, and over her arm she carried a freshly pressed apron with a flower pattern from decades ago. Adelina followed her.

The signora looked Adelina over carefully. "What do you know of chocolate? I come from a long line of women who have skills beyond what a mere amateur could hope to gain, especially from books and…" She waved off the tablet in Adelina's hands. "My great grandmother had the touch. My grandmother saved this entire village during the war with her chocolates!"

"I wasn't aware," Adelina lied. She had tied her black hair back, wore a short sleeve T-shirt that wouldn't impede her work, and sturdy shoes, ready for a day at the long table. She hadn't heard the story about the war, but her research last night had uncovered several generations of chocolatiers in Signora Liguria's line. "Well, I will find a culinary school somewhere, because I am determined—"

"Ba," Signora Liguria spat. "School! You learn with your hands, your nostrils." She narrowed her eyes at Adelina. "Your brother wants my bakery, your mother steals my son, and now you're going to compete against my chocolates? You're a family of vampires!"

"My brother has been so busy at the restaurant that he hasn't had time to think of anything else. I think the bread business is off the table."

The old woman turned her back on Adelina and moved behind the work table. "I have recipes you won't find anywhere."

"I would imagine so! I doubt I could find an apprenticeship that would train me to your level." A shameless ploy, Adelina admonished herself, but she held her ground.

Bettina sighed. The girl had talked her into a corner. So this was how Adelina's mother had ensnared her son: sly talk. Yesterday, the American had not arrived but had sent a short note in fractured Italian declining to help any further. Just as well because the American had no ability. Anyone could see—and Adelina had first-hand experience—that Bettina could not run this confectionary alone, and Bettina was worried that the girl might actually open another shop in the village. She grumbled under her breath but knew her blustering had very little merit.

And she had already started down the path—she had received large shipments of chocolate, butter, gallons of cream, expensive spices. It had awakened a creative side of her. Even an old woman needed a purpose in life, something she could do with mastery. The swirling, molten chocolate called to her. And to Adelina. Apparently, Bettina thought, Adelina had felt what she had seen in her: an aptitude, but more importantly, a love.

Bettina had been staying at the confectionary long into the evening every day, spending hours on her feet, oblivious to the pain until she got home. She had been making progress. She had deciphered the faded writing of three additional recipes of her grandmother. She worked every day to improve the uniformity of her pieces, to be sure that the walls of the molded chocolates could hold the ganache without breaking and yet not be so thick that they were nearly solid. And she had two recipes that were all her own. Besides, she had to admit, she had trouble lifting even small pans, and removing just three dozen pieces from the molds made her hands ache at the end of the day. But it would be an affront to her grandmother and the generations before her, all the way back to little Gemma who had crawled through the milk door. *You see, the first mistresses took in a chocolatier outside the bloodline. The chocolate called; the chocolate demanded it. My recipes and Adelina's techniques.* She would write letters tonight, regardless.

"I suppose I could use the help…but I don't pay you until the chocolates sell."

Adelina beamed and try to give her a little hug that Bettina awkwardly dodged.

Bettina's letters went out four at a time, with no answer. The walk to the post office and back became part of her daily routine, especially reassuring on her way home from the confectionary after watching Adelina's skills improve quicker than Bettina had expected. Adelina was young and unformed enough to follow her grandmother's recipes without question, and Bettina's instruction to the letter. She had even left her there to finish cleaning and lock up.

Adelina was exhausted from an only relatively successful round of chocolates—these were to be liqueur-filled cups, and instead they were misshapen chocolate blobs and broken vessels. Despite her fatigue, she scrubbed at the side of the work table with a kitchen towel, cleaned the smudges off the jar holding tools, and finally sat down in front of the long expanse of table.

All so different from my art. Her paintings were angry and dark, nightmares almost, and the only review she had ever received—in the back pages of an alternative paper in Rome—questioned whether she was bitter and furious. Antonio had always said that was why she never sold any work—no one wanted something so frightening hanging in their home. At first, she had been surprised by the comments, and then she believed them. She convinced herself that she was listening to what her art told her: that she was a woman who was not at peace, who was intensely enraged. And yet here she was, spending as much time as she could enveloped in this beautiful smell, peacefully working with this exquisite substance that was more monochromatic than her paints, but just as challenging and much more rewarding.

Adelina decided that it was better not to tell anyone about her new involvement with chocolate, especially as it involved the bakery. At the same time, the toll of her dual existence was wearing on her: she worked 6 a.m. to 10 a.m. in the confectionary, changed her clothes in the bakery bathroom, then rushed to the restaurant to set up for lunch, worked until three, immediately ran back to the confectionary where she swapped out a blouse for a t-shirt to continue her apprenticeship, and returned to the restaurant at six for the traditional 8 p.m. dinner seating, ushering the last guests out at 11 p.m. And because she wouldn't tell Paolo where she was going—for fear he would either ridicule her or resume his drive toward the bakery—he seemed to assume that she was sleeping or shopping, and so he was gruff with her when she left and resentful when she returned.

But she had to keep at it, especially now. Last night, Adelina had been pouring wine at a table close to the kitchen when she heard a truck pull up. Since Paolo was at the stove and her father was not at the restaurant, she knew it fell to her to investigate this late delivery of two large boxes that were set unceremoniously in the back doorway of the kitchen. The boxes came up to her knees and were wider than her hips. Her curiosity turned to anxiety as she saw the return address—her own apartment in Rome. She tore open the first box and her stomach fell at the sight of a letter from her boyfriend and the rest of her belongings. She wanted to close the box and pretend it hadn't happened, to holler and throw things around the back garden, to hide the boxes so no one could see the shameful way she had been dismissed. She was not, however, surprised. No going back, she thought.

***

Paolo sat at the family patio table wiping the sweat off his forehead as if he believed the gesture could reinvigorate exhausted thoughts. He had wanted something of his own and he was now shocked at the demands of it. The kitchen had just finished prep on time, and all he could think about was the little nap room. He was proud of himself for getting a whole menu together, (zucchini with pancetta and thyme, sea bass in parchment, lemon *sorbetto*) but still, he was stunned. The dew hadn't risen off the basil in the garden yet, the birds were still announcing morning, and already he was exhausted.

And it occurred to him how high the stakes were now: in the past, if he had failed to distinguish himself he was still second-in-command at a successful restaurant. Now, if he failed, he destroyed a legacy. And he understood that if he stayed in his father's shadow, he would always be able to claim that he was his father's equal without having to prove it, but once his father stepped aside there would be no more excuses. The feeling was far more frightening than when he contemplated the ennui of being second-in-command; it was more terrifying than the thought of having his own bakery had been exhilarating.

It was in the midst of this disconcerting realization that Paolo looked up and saw that the butchers were here with their usual delivery. The three butcher brothers were nearly the same age as Paolo, so they had all played soccer years ago and had had a few drunken misadventures. But here was someone new. A woman climbed out of the van wearing a butcher's coat dotted with blood, and a thick blonde braid hung down her shoulder to below her cleavage. He watched her haul a heavy case of meat from the back of the van. Just as she swung towards him, she saw him and fumbled, dropping one end of the case, then stopping its fall with her knee and juggling it back into position. She looked away in embarrassment and, cussing, hobbled on the injured leg. The brothers were surprised at her clumsiness, looked at her then at Paolo, and the oldest one, Roberto, looked down at the ground with a little smile.

Kate scoffed at herself but strode toward the man with mock bravado. She set the heavy box down on the table with a thud.

The man rose. Kate's breath caught in her throat. *He looks like a postcard of an Italian, GQ-at-the-palazzo.* She stepped back, tried to smooth the front of her jacket, and was suddenly embarrassed by the blood splatters. She checked her pants, took a sly look at her shoes to make sure there was no offal clinging to their sides.

This nervousness was unlike her. Men didn't throw her, especially handsome men—their vanity made them so easy to…not exactly manipulate but…handle. Today, surrounded by the aroma of the kitchen garden and the delicious smells of lunch prep—lemon, butter, beef, wine, fish—her gaze went past the handsome man into the kitchen; past the hanging rack of copper pots and the gentle sun that glinted off them; into the restaurant with its polished floors, well-worn table legs, pressed linens; and out into the center of the village whose cobblestones surrounded the base of an old fountain. She drank in the beauty of it, and as she brought her gaze back to the man, the reverberation of that beauty augmented what she saw in him.

He called to the butchers as they followed behind her with other boxes. "You have my usual order?"

"Of course," said Roberto and looked at him slyly. "And then some."

Kate knew this was her cue. "Kate Christopher, from New Zealand, the land of sheep and lamb," she said in Italian.

The man smiled at her odd accent. She offered her hand to shake. She was more comfortable now that she could deliver her sales pitch. "I know everything there is to know about lamb and mutton…so I'm bringing a line of the very finest to the area." She was having difficulty getting through her standard patter. She unwrapped a lean slab from its butcher paper. "Very tender. Grass fed." Rather than waxing poetic about the quality of the herd, the precision of the butchering, she sped forward to the end. "Let me leave you with a small sampling of ground lamb and…" She gestured toward the van and started backing away. "Give us a call, I mean…call the butcher shop and…give it a try."

So this is what stunning means—looks that paralyze and befuddle.

She backed away from the table, nearly forgetting her box of samples, then darted forward with an awkward little step and yanked it by its handles.

Paolo sensed her reaction, and it increased the heat that had risen in his blood. "You have recipes?" He had plenty of recipes, but this woman seemed alive in a wild and visceral way that he hadn't seen among the village women. He stepped toward her and looked into the box: lamb chops, leg of lamb, crown roast, and ground. "You have eye of loin?" He could see that there wasn't any in the box.

"Not with me today, no. At the shop, though. Beautifully thin and lean, though I don't currently have enough for you to put on the menu."

He shrugged in a way that he hoped would cover his excitement over meeting her. "I would want to try it first anyway. You could bring some by? Between lunch and dinner? Three o'clock?"

"Oh, that's going to be difficult." She turned back to her compatriots, but they had already retreated to the van. While she was turned, Paolo saw the butcher brothers watching from the windows, while the oldest, Roberto, leaned against the van, grinding on a toothpick to hide his smile.

Kate stammered. "We are not…back by here until…"

Roberto threw his toothpick into the dust and stepped forward in what looked to Paolo like mock protest. "What, you refuse a sale? We don't do that here. The customer wants it. You bring the van back." The other brothers pulled their heads in the window to hide their mirth.

"A sample of the loin then," she said, and hurried back to the van.

Paolo saw her wave at him as the van pulled away, and he enthusiastically waved back as if he were flagging down a bus that was leaving him behind. New Zealand. He imagined that was just the beginning of it; she had probably traveled the world. She spoke Italian? How many other languages? That alone made her delicious to him, as well as her rope-like blonde hair, her eyes. He went back to the stove but was distracted.

Paolo checked the clock repeatedly. As the lunch guests dwindled, he threw a linen over a small table in the kitchen garden. He set a good bottle of wine on the table, then decided its quality was too much of a giveaway, and so he swapped it out for one that was everyday good, not "someone special" outstanding. Nonchalance: this was key.

After he had called it off with Carlotta, he'd thought he was living a wild life. The Americans, the Japanese, and the Australians who came through the village would let him bed them and then get back on their bus or plane. That was fine for a while. He had been the envy of the men in the village (and a warning to the mothers), but after the second American sorority sister arrived with a sparkle in her eye, reciting the name of another college girl who had come through the village and been bedded quite handily, he knew he had become a vacation experience, a caricature of Italian men, so predictable that it was made part of an itinerary, and it made him feel small. He had given up on foreign women altogether. Time to reconsider, he thought.

20

Kate raised her hand to wave goodbye to Paolo, but it was an odd gesture, she thought. Half-hearted, clumsy like her speech had been, almost a flat-hand stop sign. Was he the chef or the sous chef? She asked the brothers and they described what would be his inevitable progression toward ownership of the restaurant. She didn't care about the money, but to have such a clear vision of his future— what she wouldn't give for that.

Kate watched Paolo in the side view mirror as the van pulled away and, though he was smaller on the horizon, her connection to him grew deeper. He had the life she knew she needed: rooted, consistent; a deep, warm familiarity with every street, door hinge, steeple, and cobblestone; a story that came from his own life at every street corner; memories of childhood and adolescence through every archway. That was the way it was in these little villages, wasn't it? Her own peripatetic life was shallow by comparison. It wasn't that it was dull, it was just that the inconsistency of it made her weary: even a barrage of good things could take its toll.

The daughter of a New Zealand diplomat, Kate had gone through elementary school in four different countries, but when given the choice to go to a boarding school in New Zealand while her parents continued their international sojourn, she had chosen to go with them. It was, essentially, a choice between consistency of affection or consistency in landscape. She wasn't always sure that she had chosen wisely. The natural pulling-away from parents of the teenage years gave her nowhere to go but into the wilds of a foreign country, so she had vacillated between being overly-attached or too wild in her behavior— there were no small steps, like a solo venture for ice cream in the cafe where the family went every Sunday (a remarkable story that she had heard from an Irish girl when they were stationed in Dublin). Wild swings of behavior left her with a deep sense of being unmoored. That had been her childhood.

Paolo's restaurant was the last stop before they turned the van around and headed back to the butcher shop two villages away. Her colleagues made short work of the end of their day, which was the midafternoon. Kate checked the lamb loin for flaws but put it back on the refrigerator shelf. The others were hanging up their aprons and scrubbing their hands, but even though Kate had somewhere to go, she stood in the middle of the butchering room. She would clean the saws, she said, surprising the brothers. She wanted to scrub out the walk-in refrigerator and it had to be done today, she protested.

She arrived 40 minutes late, pulling up beside the restaurant and braking so fast that the van threw up dust. She bounded into the back garden, and when Paolo stood, freshly showered and in a clean linen shirt, she was embarrassed by her own appearance. She had washed her hands before she left the butcher shop, but she still wore the sweaty and bloodstained clothes from scrubbing the equipment, and there was no doubt that her face was salty with sweat. Why was she so flustered? Suddenly she remembered that she had left the lamb loin in the cooler in the back of the van, so she excused herself and backed away. She scrubbed at her face with a packaged wipe and scolded herself for arriving with no makeup, in a state like this.

She returned, and he handed her a glass of red wine which she exchanged for the wrapped meat. He motioned her into the kitchen, where he unwrapped the lamb and laid it gently on the cutting board next to the stove. She could see through the archway that the last guests were leaving, the busboy wiping tables and setting up for dinner.

"A marinade." Paolo said it gently but with authority. "Mint, thyme, garlic of course. It's very lean."

"Yes. Should we roll it?"

"Good. Tied, seared, baked. Let's give it a minute in the marinade."

They sat at the little table in the garden and Kate started to relax. He complimented her on her Italian. She shook her head in a humble way and didn't mention her three other languages. *Here comes the awkward part*, she thought. *Where did I grow up? Oh my, so many schools, so many countries, and my family from the upper class.* She dreaded it. Yet in the past, if she omitted any of the details, she was accused of withholding. Worse yet, when she revealed her sense of lonely drifting she would be given the "poor little rich girl" look. But she and Paolo talked about food, cooking. She described sheep farming, the rollicking parties after shearing—though she had only participated twice before her family was off to another destination. Had they been en route to Kenya that time?

They told stories and laughed, drained the bottle of wine, made themselves the butt of their own jokes, jumped up to describe the odd postures and ridiculous gestures in a story, recounted adventures with abandon. Back in the kitchen, Kate stood near him as he seared the lamb, admired the speed with which he cut vegetables, was attentive as he lifted the copper lid on the polenta and deemed it worthy of reconstitution. They walked the perimeter of the garden and he pointed out the herbs. She told him of the herbs in the garden in Morocco, how she'd longed for it when they had lived in Helsinki. He was impressed by her travels, he said. But when she mentioned the feeling of drifting he looked at her kindly, extended his sympathy, cupped her elbow in his hand for a moment. It was a kindness that brought a flush to her cheeks.

When they returned to the kitchen, Paolo suggested they make *zabaglione*, and that she should do the whipping. He splashed ingredients into the bowl she held in her arms. Whip it faster, he ordered, laughing. Then—emboldened by the wine or his desire for her, she wondered and hoped—he stepped behind her, seizing her hand with the whisk until they were splashing it around the kitchen and themselves.

After they had consumed every trifle they could think of that might prolong the afternoon, the conversation hit a satisfied, though not awkward lull. The dinner seating would be soon and the (newly promoted) sous chef interrupted with questions more frequently. Kate said her goodbyes.

The next morning, however, she tried to put the afternoon out of her mind and was all business again. She couldn't blame it on the wine—they hadn't consumed that much—but she regretted having gone to the restaurant, and as she and the butcher's sons loaded up the van for the day's deliveries, she gave them a careful list but refused to join them.

***

While making the *zabaglione*, Paolo had wanted to hold her, to scoop her up and take her home. Instead, he'd spooned the custard into small glasses and led her back into the garden.

He had shaved carefully in the morning, and kept replaying the memory in his head, was disappointed when she didn't arrive, but he kept it to himself. He made a point of ordering lamb, but the next day it arrived without her. After a week, Paolo decided she was one of those women who are tourists no matter how long they stay. They were "enchanted" with the village as if it were a theme park, he thought angrily.

Early in the morning about a week and a half after their dinner, Paolo convinced himself he was just continuing his quest for a new source of bread when he went to the village with the butcher shop. He had forgotten that the bakery was directly across the street from the butcher shop and that it was a very narrow street. He tried to keep his back to the butcher shop and only looked toward it when he was inside the bakery with the case and counter between him and the front window. He told himself it was good business to ask so many questions about the bakery's capacity before he had even tasted the bread and rolls, only half-listening to the answers as he looked toward the butcher's hoping for a glimpse of her. He bought a small baguette and a roll and stood outside next to the bakery breaking them apart, checking their consistency.

He had just bitten into the roll and was so intently staring into the little paper bag that he didn't immediately see Kate come around the corner toward the butcher shop. Seeing him, she stopped. She crossed the street, but when she reached him, she fumbled over her words, then put her hands on her hips.

"Let's have supper again," she said.

He tried to keep the relief from showing on his face. "Breakfast is easier for me. How about now?" When she smiled, Paolo took her hand and walked her to the bodega in the town square.

"I almost didn't recognize you," he said. "You're so clean."

She laughed. "That's why I crossed the street—I'm unrecognizable without the blood spatters."

They ordered small dishes in slow succession, their jokes becoming more personal but just as funny. Kate's hair was braided, her V-neck shirt was clean, and her jeans were tight. Finally, she announced that it was time for her to go to work and she stood up, fumbled in her purse for money.

Paolo stood and stopped her from retrieving any cash but continued to hold her fist. He brought her hand to his mouth. He kissed the soft flesh between her thumb and first finger. "Come to the restaurant tonight at closing. It's late but…" he whispered. She breathed deeply and after a bit of consideration, nodded her head slightly.

***

When she arrived, the last customer had gone, and the busboy was pouring the mop water out to finish his shift. This time, Kate came in through the front of the restaurant, in a sky-blue dress and sandals, her thick and shining hair loose around her shoulders. Paolo was without his apron, she noticed and as he handed her a glass of red wine, he slid his hand up her neck and pulled her forward to kiss her. With more grace than she had exhibited previously, she got the glass to the bar without spilling it and responded to his advance. He pressed her against the bar and he ran his hands through her hair, guiding her head through the long, complex kiss. He led her to the daybed in the little room between the restaurant and kitchen, and they made love until they were exhausted.

***

She returned the following night and most nights thereafter. They hurried through small plates, went into the nap room earlier, and still managed to get Kate home in time to get a little sleep before work. Sometimes they slept late and had breakfast together in a remote bar in the village. One morning over breakfast, Paolo invited her to come to the restaurant, but this time, before closing.

"You can meet my sister. Maybe my father will show up." He didn't say what he was thinking though: that the thought of her cheered him, that being with her gave more meaning to his life, began to restore his hope for love.

Kate was a different type of woman, he reasoned. True, she had just bounced into town, but when they talked late into the night, holding hands, she seemed to really appreciate the little things she saw in the village. She seemed sincere. She wanted to move somewhere that was quiet, she had said. His heart opened a little more every day. Maybe here was someone who was the best combination of worldly and willing to live in the village, who was beautiful and worthy of Paris and Rome, and yet wanted a straightforward and predictable village life.

He tried not to grasp at it as his last chance for love. He tried not to seem too thirsty for it. He made love in a measured way to obscure his hungry desire for connection. He tried to keep from getting ahead of himself and dreaming about their children, or how he might buy the house on the far edge of the village that overlooked the valley. He tried to work without letting his giddiness distract him, and to keep the lust from his face so the bus boy and the butchers wouldn't see it. And especially so he could hide it from his father, who Paolo imagined was dog paddling through his loss, if he ever surfaced.

"Just come by," he said to Kate. "No need to hide anymore."

As Paolo drew closer to her over the café table with his suggestion of a family gathering, Kate was overcome with a desire to run away. Hop a boat, book a ticket. He reached near her for salt and pepper and she saw the airport departures board. As he slid his hand over hers, she heard the wheels of her suitcase rolling across a moving walkway.

"We'll see." She swallowed and would not meet his eyes.

She showed up to work moving at double speed. She volunteered to use the bandsaw. *Paolo is fun, but now it's becoming something different. Dear God, meet his family?* She shuddered. She wasn't the type.

She saw people in the market living like that—debating together over which apple to choose. *Olive bread or baguettes? How wide should the ham be? Which fragrance of soap? What side of the street to walk on? Take the car or the bus?* Who could stand being boxed in hip-to-hip? Stifling, all these joint decisions on topics unworthy of the energy it took to make them. *The width of ham? Not for me*, she thought in a panic. This was just a question of lifestyle. Some people were made for collective life. She was not.

She slapped cuts of meat on the sideboard of the grinder before her colleagues could take the position. Part of her was in a dead panic; part of her was sad. This hadn't worked out. Close, but not really. She had a friend in Germany who was opening an art gallery and might need some help. Yes, that was it.

***

Paolo was surprised when she didn't show up that evening during business hours. Luckily, he hadn't told his sister about her or he'd be humiliated on top of being disappointed. Still, it was rude. He sent the cleaning staff home early and was mopping the floor himself when she walked in. He chose not to speak.

"Sorry, I couldn't get here sooner. I have a lot to do before catching the plane in the morning."

Paolo looked at her with a rapidly hardening scowl. "Where are you going?"

"Berlin."

21

Dario sat in the sun on the park bench trying to untangle the mess of his marriage. He and his wife had both grown up in this village and, even as a child, Rosa had had a faraway look in her eyes, a searching quality. When they were teenagers, it had excited Dario: he had thought it was desire.

It propelled them toward marriage, and when his parents died and he took over the restaurant, he thought her look was toward the future, his success, their impending prosperity. It had driven him to work hard, change the menu, go from a little café that was visited because there was no other, to a destination, a restaurant people drove uphill to frequent. Wealthy landowners on horseback stopped in by chance and, surprised by the quality of their lunch, brought their friends, who then brought people from Rome—who called it quaint and authentic and, when it became popular, bemoaned the fact that it started getting busy. Dario had given them a false little smile because he thought it was rude to say that his success undermined their panache.

But he was successful, and in part, it was to dampen the faraway, hungry look on Rosa's face. He could give her what she needed to be satisfied, not just in bed but in all parts of her life. When she was pregnant with each child, he assumed the look was the desire for the child and then for a secure future for them; when her second pregnancy ended in a miscarriage, he believed her look was grief. The restaurant fell out of favor when a wealthy wine merchant sold his villa and moved back to Rome; and the look in her eyes drove him to court favor with the locals, travel to all the nearby towns joining business groups and welcoming birthday parties. Now, it was astounding to him how much he had been driven by the wistful look in her eyes. What if her focus on the future had been insatiable? Was her running off with the baker just another way to keep her eyes on the horizon? He put his head in his hands, and when he lifted it, he was even more enraged than he had been before. She had led him along like an ox with a ring in his nose, and his jealousy over the arrival of another man now mixed with relief that he was suddenly un-yoked, that he was free of her insatiability.

But the seesaw began again: he was not only cuckolded in his marriage bed (by an older man!), but if her desire had been driving their life, she had usurped his own sense of self, his position as master of his own fate. Had he been deluded all along? How could he walk through the village like a man, especially like a man of stature? *Enough of this*, he thought. He was done with her.

He marched back to the restaurant with more determination and energy than he had displayed since she had left, growled at the dishwasher, but refused to meet his son's eyes when Paolo arrived with a box of mushrooms and 14 eggplants. Dario worked feverishly, but his anger gave him a precision that resulted in browned chops sweet and moist, sauces with perfectly balanced flavors, all delivered to a table piping hot, glistening, and on time.

Yet as the evening wore on, Dario found himself looking over at the end bar stool, wondering about the brokenhearted, chestnut-haired American. He saved the last lamb chop with olives and onions for her, set aside enough ingredients for a last *zabaglione*. But before closing, with no sign of her, he dismissively gave the food to the sous chef.

The next morning, Dario was there earlier than usual and invented half of the menu on the fly. Paolo still refused to speak to him.

During a break, Dario stood with his hands flat on the bar looking at the little hotel where Gretchen lived. When was the last time she had been seen? He asked the kitchen staff, and they shrugged. At noon, he plated the day's specials and put them on a tray. Little Marco was sitting on the edge of the central fountain, and Dario called to him. Just as he was handing the tray to the child with instructions to take it to Gretchen, Luca walked up to the hotel with a bouquet of flowers. Dario yanked the tray away from the child and angrily set it down on the bar again, fuming over his own foolishness.

But when Luca reappeared, flowers still in his hand, Dario was even more worried about Gretchen. He barked at Marco to come back and Dario thrust the tray into his hands again.

"Give this to the American and ask when she ate last…but report to me at the back door." His tone was terse and harsh, belying the concern he felt.

Within three minutes, the little boy was at the back door of the restaurant, but he was still holding the tray with all its contents. "She's there but won't come out, won't open the door. Signor Giordano, I tried."

"You're sure she hasn't left?" Had she been locked in her room while he had wandered the village?

"They say they hear her crying, and sometimes they hear the shower, but no one has seen her in days."

"Where is she, which room?"

"The balcony room."

Dario took the tray from the boy, but when the child looked up at Dario with hunger, he gave it back to him and motioned to the courtyard. Marco ate with gusto.

Dario thought best standing at the stove, and so he worried the onions and fresh oregano until they nearly scorched. With the leg of lamb browned, tied in juniper berries and rosemary and in the oven, he took a flat box, draped the bottom with a napkin, put in a small covered dish of risotto with mushrooms, added a peach, and covered it all with another napkin. He took off his apron and hesitated over the box, then saw Paolo's sideways, disapproving glance. Dario left by the back door, through the gate. He walked into the hotel through the kitchen and, passing behind the empty proprietress's station, snatched the key from its hook and took the stairs two at a time.

"Signora. Gretchen. Open the door." When there was no reply, it heightened Dario's fear for her. He glanced around the hall to make sure he was alone, and he quietly slipped the key into the lock. Entering, he set the box on the side table but remained close to the door. "Gretchen," he said breathlessly, pegging the arousing woman in front of him with his memory of her in his arms at the wall.

She rolled over as she threw back the covers and stood still for only a moment before she walked toward him, not bothering to cinch her pale blue robe.

"Comforting me again?" she asked quietly.

Dario met her halfway and cupped the back of her head with his right hand as he pulled her toward him, and settled his left hand in the downy small of her back. Her breasts were large and firm, her skin pale but inviting. They made love all afternoon, voracious and then tender. They fell asleep in each other's arms.

When Dario left, they agreed—through halting English and the clumsy assistance of her iPhone translator—that it would be better to keep this to themselves for fear of the villagers' opinions and his wife's potential use of it in the divorce. Dario wrestled with what was expected of him, but also wondered what Gretchen might like for lunch the following day.

***

Gretchen languidly strolled through the narrow, crooked streets of the village, more relaxed than she had been since long before her son had died. Her hair was swept onto the top of her head, and a new lime-green dress stroked her thighs when she walked. She tried to calculate if she had enough money from her divorce settlement to stay in the hotel or if she would have to rent an apartment somewhere else in town. Was she prepared to sell her house? That seemed a very drastic measure. But what about her bright yellow room, the restaurant, the soothing sound of the fountain?

And Dario. She and Dario had been making love out of town at little inns, late at night in secret in her hotel room. And once, even deep in the forest after a picnic. It didn't matter that they had no language in common: in a way, it was part of what made it work. She didn't have to explain what had happened or how she had reacted, recount stories of the past, relive the fumbling around in her grief. They had a wordless companionship and comfort (unless there was the necessity to bring out the phone, which they only did for very practical conversations). It was foolishness anyway, the two of them becoming lovers, and since there wasn't any way to explain it, there wasn't any need for words to explain it. Reveling in the sensuality of time with Dario was a relief from her pain. That was enough, wasn't it? She had failed at bread and chocolate, stumbled into blinding grief a few times, and taken a lover. She wondered if her sister would consider that progress.

She circled back to the fountain near her hotel. Seeing the restaurant filling with locals who laughed with Adelina and Dario, she beamed with joy at him.

Seeing her, Dario turned his back.

The gesture cut her to the core, made her feel that he was ashamed of her, of them. She moved to the far side of the fountain away from the restaurant and sat with her legs out in front of her. After the first sting of it, though, she knew he was right. She pulled her legs in, pressed her knees together, as if her posture could foster a more practical attitude. Even if she became fluent in Italian—an extremely unlikely possibility since she was not very talented with languages—she doubted she would be fluent enough to become jocular with Dario's customers. She didn't have the background and history that made their relationships so comfortable. And she doubted it would improve in the short run: from what she had seen of their reaction to the baker and Dario's wife, the villagers would never approve of her living with Dario or openly being his mistress, and she certainly was in no state for marriage. The thought of it made her shudder. Lacking a common language hadn't ruled out a tryst, but it certainly undermined the foundation for a relationship.

Besides, since the first time he came to her room, she had been dreaming of her home on Loon Lake. Since Nate died, her dreams had been dark, paralyzing labyrinths. Though waking was little better, at least she knew it was real and that the laws of physics limited the arrival of macabre faces and the crush of dark walls. In these new dreams, she and someone she couldn't see—but who sometimes held her hand—slowly walked a sandy lane with an arch of birch trees overhead. Instead of morosely plodding, their steps were light, occasionally veering off and twirling in the sand. Each night in the dream they walked further, until one night they reached a bend in the road and she realized that it was the path to the elementary school. In the morning, sitting in bed with coffee, she was perplexed: it had clearly involved Nate, but it had been a happy dream.

The last time she had slept in Dario's arms she had woken in the night, convinced she was smelling the moss and hearing the gurgle of the creek beside her yard. This morning, Gretchen had awakened to a sound like loons after dreaming of flying across the surface of the lake. She had gotten into the shower longing for home, the moist night air of Loon Lake and the rustle of poplar leaves.

But to go back to Loon Lake—it was the theater her grief played in, wasn't it? Could her dreams be trusted? Could she live there without her little boy? The blissful times with Dario that held her grief at bay for hours made her wonder if the grief was the only thing that still connected her to her little boy. After all these months of wishing that the pain would subside, she now almost wanted to fall back into it for fear that, without the pain, she would forget who Nate had been and how much she had loved him. Impossible, she thought. Initially, when Nate had died, she had turned away from her husband Bob. Nate had had Bob's ears, and he had her eyes; people had said so for years and, like so many other parents, they couldn't see it, until Nate was gone. The sight of those little glimpses of him had stung them. Then it switched direction, as if they had gotten it all from Nate. Bob's goofy ears—prominent in Nate's kindergarten photos—were now almost reassurance that some part of their little boy still existed. A gift from him.

She dipped her hand into the fountain. Was she going to give up all of this, Dario, the village? To do what? Go live again in a place where Kate's Country Kitchen served honey-stung chicken on Monday and perch on Friday? Beer from faux pickle jars? Would she go back to organizing the paperwork of the local hardware store? Yes. She knew the answer was yes. It would be painful to drive by the school were Nate had been, but she realized that at this point, she couldn't compare her situation to the life she would have had. That was gone without a trace. Now the only question was whether she would surround herself with the memories of him or live in a place with no trace of him, as if he had never existed. True, crossing paths with the schoolchildren had reduced her to tears and days in bed, but there was no place in the world without children, and rather than seeing the ghost of her son in places he had never been, wouldn't she rather relish actual memories? If she didn't return, would she be willing to never see the yard where he had played, never go by the ice cream stand and remember him smeared with sherbet, never drive by the park and see him on the swings, jumping off with abandon? The huckleberry patch; the end of the dock. That's what her choice had been reduced to: memories or a void. Running away had seemed easier but was worse in the end.

She had to go back. But her dearest, luscious Dario. She would write him a letter with her translation app, go by the restaurant in the morning, leave the following day. It would be too painful to draw it out any further.

***

Dario went back to the stove with a heavy heart. He had turned away from Gretchen, to hide her, to hide *them*—he had always thought that he was not that kind of man. They had never discussed when her vacation was scheduled to end, and he felt as if he was betraying her to wonder about it now, to have edged away from her the first time they were seen near each other in public. He could never introduce Gretchen to his children. There was no place for her in the restaurant. But her beautiful lips, her breasts in his hands. It had been a fling; any man would have done it. That was no consolation, he thought. He just hoped he didn't hurt her in the end.

22

Luca sat in the bakery in one of the two flowered chairs opposite the work table, clearly not registering Adelina's embarrassment over having someone else in the bakery when she fell under the trance of the chocolate. Especially Mr. Lump of Coal.

Adelina began tempering chocolate, but every time she moved from one end of the table to the next, she looked up to see Luca and was intrigued. He was reading a book; Adelina had never seen her boyfriend read anything other than men's fashion magazines. Other contrasts with her boyfriend were just as surprising to her; Luca's his feet barely touched the floor while he sat; his head came up to the middle of the high-back chair. But he was burnished and manly. Substantive. Warm. His clothing was a little out of date, though classic, as if he had paid attention to fashion one year and then checked the topic off his list. It probably couldn't even be considered a wardrobe. Belt—check. Jacket—check. One shirt for work, one for chores, one for church. It was refreshing. And with the aroma of the chocolate enveloping her, Adelina felt drawn to him, to the quietude of him, to what she imagined would be steadfast kindness, to the surety of a walk hand-in-hand down a street she knew. He seemed genuine, trustworthy, even though he was there looking for the American that Adelina had heard about but never met.

She started experimenting with fillings and ingredients, changing what she was doing based on his reaction—whether he shifted in his chair, or lifted his chin to inhale. When he threw his head back and closed his eyes, she knew she had selected correctly. Limoncello ganache. She mixed it in quantity and he settled deeper into his chair. She smiled.

Adelina looked at Luca hunched over his book. Signora Liguria would be pleased with her output; there were a few extra. It took her two hours, but she made a full tray of rose-shaped dark chocolate pieces with piped-in limoncello ganache.

Luca considered his options. He had been told at the hotel that the American was unreachable, and at the bakery, Adelina told him that she hadn't been showing up to work. Luca had pulled a paperback out of his coat pocket and settled in to wait for Gretchen, or for his next move to come to him. Luca continued reading, looking at Adelina when she was looking down at the table. He hadn't seen her in years, not since her move to Rome. His gaze lingered on her neck and her strong, bare arms. Was he honestly searching for a glimpse of her cleavage behind her apron? The courage he had gathered to approach Gretchen now emboldened him in appreciating young, lithe, lovely Adelina. But he chided himself: it seemed more logical to approach the American. Because she would leave soon? Well, he could look, and Adelina was gorgeous.

Adelina wrapped four chocolates in a napkin, removed her apron, blotted her face with a small towel, and tried to straighten her hair. She walked toward Luca with the napkin, and she seemed to be becoming more excited with every step—no, he was flattering himself.

"I thought you might like these."

Luca looked at the chocolates and his face warmed. Was it that obvious that he had designs on the American? So obvious that the local chocolatier made up batches for him in advance? "Thank you. How much do I owe you?"

"No, no. These are for…you." Adelina became flustered. "You seemed to…like the aroma." She gestured back toward the kitchen.

Luca held the small handful, feeling awkward about his assumption that he could give these chocolates to Gretchen. And he certainly knew what discomfort looked like, what it felt like to be rebuffed or misunderstood—just the way Adelina was standing here now—so he fumbled for words.

"Please," he gestured for her to sit in the other chair beside him, "tell me about your chocolates."

Adelina put her hands up. "They are more for enjoying than discussing."

Luca wanted to continue the conversation, though he was afraid to consider what was at the heart of his request for fear of ruining it. He gestured to the chair again.

"Some limoncello to go with this," she said, scurrying back to the kitchen and pouring two aperitif glasses with the bright yellow liqueur. "Tell me about your book." She smoothed her skirt under her legs as she sat.

Murder mysteries? They were her guilty pleasure as well. This author in particular? She had four novels beside her bed. (*In Rome, though now probably in the bottom of one of the delivered boxes.*) He never went anywhere without one in his pocket. She smiled. He grinned. She was a painter? How ambitious, how talented, he praised her; he had no abilities like that, he admitted. Tomatoes and basil? She envied his ability to grow them in his yard. He was maybe a dozen years older than her and unlike anyone she had ever known, but she wanted to crawl inside his coat, fold herself into his lap. *Of course you won't*, she reprimanded herself, but she was unable to explain the desire.

"Which one is this?" Luca pointed at the clutch of chocolates now on the table between them. She described the liqueur, the process, tentatively explaining her newly-acquired avocation. She lit up at the look on his face as he savored the ganache. Not a swoon like a woman, or a gourmand's muted response, but a very sexual grunt. He closed his eyes, turned his head ever so slightly.

Adelina looked down at her lap in sudden surprise at herself. She never would have met Luca in one of the clubs that she and Antonio had worked so hard to get into on a Saturday night. And yet there was safety in her feelings for Luca. This was an affection or a desire completely outside the rest of her life, which gave it a purity. To have failed with someone as handsome as Antonio or to have fallen in love with someone as shallow as Antonio—both sides of the argument made her miserable. But Luca was a man of substance, a solid, kind man. She tried to get a grip on herself as he announced his departure and she showed him to the door.

***

Luca clutched the chocolates in his pocket as he walked back toward his car. He recalled the warmth of Adelina's expression. The surprise of such a gift. *Could that have been pleasure on her face? Could it have been... desire?* He immediately checked himself. *And what about the American?* His enchantment with Adelina had driven Gretchen from his mind.

When was the last time he had been desired? Grammar school? Just after secondary school, he had gone to Rome with friends and there had been a blonde who had gotten drunk and fallen all over him, her slightly sweaty arm flung over his shoulder. She had drunkenly brought her face close to his, kissed him with a sticky lipstick mouth. It had been exhilarating to have his arm around her waist, to feel the flesh on her rib cage, the curve where waist turned to hip. She was very thin, her breasts mere suggestions under her dress, the puffy sleeves and narrow shoulders of which suggested a girl, an innocent, not a woman who could toss back shots like a sailor, as this woman could. In the morning, all the guys he had traveled with wrote off the women from the previous night as whores or foreigners, and he had filed the information of her away in his mind as a biology lesson, as information but not experience, as something that had nothing to do with him and, even worse, something attached to the shame of having believed any part of it for any time at all. When had anyone who was sober, anyone he would bring home to his mother, moved closer to be near him unless there was too little room on the bus? He had to dig deep into the back of his mind to even remember what the gesture looked like.

Luca drove faster than usual back to his cottage, a functional, sparse building close to the carpentry shop his brother owned. Was he misreading all this? Adelina was so young and thin, beautiful eyes, everything symmetric and unflawed. Of course she wasn't interested in him, he grumbled to himself. Then, noting that he was squealing around the mountain corners, he slowed down, turned on his high beams, and tried to get himself under control. Not in a million years would a woman that beautiful fall for him, and he was an idiot to think she would, a laughingstock if he acknowledged it. Besides, it was too late now. He had spent too many years as a bachelor, having his way, living in his own disarray. And he liked it that way, he reassured himself, slapping his palm on the steering wheel. He had his friends, his soccer games, his cigars and whiskey with his brother. People knew him. He didn't need a woman in his life, he didn't need to be married and children always seemed more work than they were worth. Other men in their group who had found girlfriends would show up late to the card games, and then didn't arrive at all. He saw them in the market, carrying the basket while she selected the produce. That just wasn't a life for him.

His palms were sweating, and he gripped the steering wheel tightly to compensate. *Not everyone is cut out for marriage. Not every bachelor wants to live any other way.* And then he thought of the American. And how happy it had made him to watch Gretchen enjoy the scenery out his car window. He wasn't interested either way. Not in the American, and not in Adelina, who couldn't be interested in him, not really. *And if she wasn't, what kind of game was she playing? Testing to see if she still had allure? Dangling her beauty in front of the local troll? Was it a pity flirt? The model and the Lump of Coal?* Luca felt an anger building in his chest. Driving home, every woman on the billboards scoffed at him, their seductive eyes and full lips more clearly a trap then he had realized before; every happy family in milk and bread ads taunted him, self-righteous and proud of excluding him. He ground his teeth. He skidded to a stop in front of his house and slammed every door his hand touched.

***

The next day, Adelina arrived earlier than usual to the confectionary, set up faster, and worked head down, almost willing herself to ignore the idea of Luca. Signora Liguria busied herself making coffee and peering over Adelina's shoulder.

With the molds set up for the day's work, Adelina smoothed her apron over her tight jeans as if it would give her courage. "We have racks and racks of chocolates." The ganache roses covered two large pans in the baker's rack. Squares of caramel waited for their small wrappers. They were a little short on the liqueur-filled half-domes. "I think we should box them up and sell them."

Signora Liguria muttered under her breath and turned away to stare at the brewing coffee. She turned back to Adelina but would not meet her eyes. "We need a name, a label." Signora Liguria gestured in the air as if there was a swirling mass of impediments. "A menu." She turned away again.

Knowing these were not insurmountable, Adelina protested, "You have a name!"

"No!" Signora Liguria was surprisingly vehement. "Not my husband's. Not my son's." She wagged a gnarled finger at Adelina.

"Fine, a name that suits you. But we should sell what we have."

"There is no 'we' here."

Adelina was offended. She took off her apron and balled it up on the work table. As Adelina stormed out, Signora Liguria called to her, but without her previous ferocity. "Besides, we'll need boxes!"

Adelina stayed away from the confectionary for several days and devoted her time to her father's restaurant. Paolo quizzed her on where she had been and nodded appreciatively when she described the chocolate operation. *Was that envy in his eyes?* Adelina wondered. She'd expected derision, or at least Paolo's usual condescension. Instead, he asked how it was to work with Signora Liguria and Adelina rolled her eyes but said nothing.

Paolo wiped his hands on his apron. "Bread is boring anyway." He turned back to the stove.

On the third day without Adelina, Signora Liguria carried a small bag to the *trattoria*. Standing with her head barely cresting the level of the bar, she laid out three boxes of ascending size. Adelina set plates down in front of customers and then stood behind the bar.

"They arrived today," Signora Liguria said. "We'll sell the chocolates in the morning. See who comes." She caught Dario's eye, quickly turned away, and headed back to the confectionary.

Adelina mentioned to the restaurant patrons that the chocolates would be available in the morning. They were enthusiastic, demanding explanations of her involvement, effusive in their praise as if she were a child. Just before closing, Luca tentatively came in and clambered up onto a barstool. Adelina was surprised to see him and asked him brightly for his order. His hair was tidier than usual, and he was freshly shaven, wearing a bit too much cologne.

Luca fumbled, realizing that in all his preparations he hadn't thought of something he could order with nonchalance. He gestured toward the cool evening air. "Limoncello." They both smiled.

As she poured it into the small glass she quietly told him the news. "Tomorrow. The chocolates are for sale starting tomorrow. If all goes well…" She shrugged her shoulders, but her eyes were anxious.

A new devotion built in Luca' chest. Was she going to stay if they sold? Work in the shop with Signora Liguria? Regardless of whether Adelina was interested in him he wanted her to stay, to come home. *Don't pretend*, Luca admonished himself. He wanted a chance.

Luca set a couple of bills under the glass and waved to her as he left. He had come back to see if he had been mistaken the other day, or maybe to see if he could be around her without acting like a fool. She had leaned in closely, spoken privately. Her citrusy cologne was light and made him taste the *limoncello* all over again. Her neck was hypnotic. He jingled coins in his pocket as he paced back down the hill toward his car.

The next morning, Luca rose early with a renewed sense of purpose. He showered and shaved, then flipped through the phone numbers of his regular clients while he was still in his boxers. Would the old widow in the next village that he drove to the doctor's office like a ride to the new chocolatier? He lined up six women, two teachers—a discounted rate, he said. He called his soccer buddies and brusquely told them he would pick them up in the late morning.

***

Adelina was on edge as she stood behind the counter. The chocolates were in precise rows, glistening, each almost exactly the same (but not exactly, she noted, and they didn't reveal how many left behind in the kitchen had cracks or extra blobs, misshapen sides, unwanted puddles instead of small, precise pedestals). She was startled by the door. The village priest, Padre Pietro, was beaming as he came in. Adelina hadn't seen him in years, and she was surprised by how wrinkled and old he looked. He called to Signora Liguria who clapped her hands in glee when she saw him. Bless us, Father, she asked, and even Adelina lowered her head in prayer. The signora boxed up several and refused payment from him. As Padre Pietro left the store, Signora Liguria stood close to Adelina behind the counter, and slipped her hand into the girl's. She looked up at Adelina with gratitude and gave her a tiny smile.

Adelina fervently wanted the chocolates to be a success, but what would it mean to her life if they were? There was little time for contemplation, though, as the greengrocer arrived and bought four roses and two of the liqueur-filled cups. She was followed by the butcher, the postman, the regulars from her father's restaurant, and then little groups of the old, the infirm, and the wealthy whom she didn't know. They came sporadically, four at a time, with short breaks in between. An old woman with a cane lingered a long time over her decision. A friend nudged her. "Luca is waiting."

"Luca?" Adelina asked.

The old woman leaned closer. "Free rides to get here today."

Adelina handed them their boxes and smiled. A thoughtful man. A humble, considerate, and giving man. She was filled with warmth as she looked down at the dwindling stock in the case. "Tell him I'll save him some."

23

Kate was edgy when the train gained speed, as if she had just dodged something, like a spot on the lung that turns out to be a spot on the lens. *Really,* she chastised herself. *Love is cancer?* All she owned was in the luggage bin above her, and that was manageable. Paolo was beautiful, and it had been delicious, but she was embarrassed that she had given into the impulse for romance, she reasoned. And yet she knew she was lying to herself and she was even more discomfited by the lie.

The Berlin trip did not make her feel better. She wandered down streets she didn't know, too late at night, too frequently fueled by bourbon. She avoided friends. If men asked her to dance, she left the club. People seemed cold, aloof, bitter, and bored. The first time she called Paolo, he hardly said a word, and she was evasive as well. The second time she called him, late at night, he was tight-lipped, but he tersely suggested that she return.

She took the late-night train to Amsterdam. It wasn't an empty life:

it was sparse. Clean. Unencumbered. Her separateness was reassuring. She avoided Italian restaurants. She didn't eat much of anything at all. She thought about returning to her parents and even called them, but hung up before speaking.

A streamlined life was good for her work, she reasoned, which immediately started an internal tirade. What work? She had left the butcher shop with hardly a word (and they had been so kind to take her on) and selling meat hardly counted as a life's work. The truth was that she had nothing for herself, no art, no commerce, home, spouse or kids. She was unmoored, and had been for the five years since college. What did she have to show for it? And that wasn't even the main question, was it? Accomplishments? Unnecessary. Suddenly she was filled with rage toward her parents. Her trust fund had made it unnecessary to work, and their self-absorption meant that they had never trained her for anything; their wandering lifestyle made it impossible for her to settle down. Suddenly jobs and achievements seemed like luxuries, things that people complain about without understanding the solidity they gave them, the sense of purpose, the structure. And, of course, it was just a *sense* of purpose, since most were involved in things that had no purpose. (Her friends in Bhutan would argue that all of it had no purpose, but she refused to consider this today.)

No, the central question was whether she was willing to live a loveless life. The thought of it frightened her, and yet the thought of love made her stomach turn. Love felt like entrapment; lovelessness like being adrift.

It needed to be the right person; no sense moving on anything until it was, she thought. And the internal rebuttal was swift and sharp. She could love Paolo, no question. She did love Paolo, but she was a coward. That was the long and short of it. She had always been a coward. She had never stayed at a job for fear of proving herself incapable, and she lacked the courage to expose herself to love.

Because that was the hard part, the essence of love. Everyone thought about the companionship, the sex, the gratification of finding someone similar or who thought you were beautiful, but love was more about being able to apologize. Love was exposure. To divulge the crap, the utter sludge of who you were, to admit that you did it (and there were so many things that could be "it") because you were broken, that despite your sleek lines and adult dress you were really just a girl whose growth stopped on a supposedly bucolic afternoon at the hands of someone who was cruel and cunning in words or deeds. Something had gone awry and you spent the rest of your life either trying to make up for it or pretend it hadn't happened. What power that event had. But what was the event in her case? She knew, but didn't want to know.

Her parents had been at the door, ready to leave. She had known they were going—and going without her—but she was stunned by the sight of them, shoulder to shoulder, pulled together in coordinated traveling clothes. Their top-shelf luggage was well packed; her mother was wearing her sensible shoes with her traveling purse that zipped closed. She could remember the feeling of sudden comprehension and surprise: they were really going to leave her behind. She recalled the presence of the housekeeper standing behind her, ready to take her to the train to boarding school. She had been entrusted to a perfunctory employee. Her parents were happy and smiling, nonplussed. And so she was the one who changed her mind. She would go with them, everywhere they went, for another decade. All her running (in the middle of the night, unannounced, that was her favorite exit plan—it was unlike her to stop by Paolo's to say goodbye), all of her leaving was to keep her from acknowledging that it hadn't been okay for them to go without her. She had to keep leaving to avoid acknowledging what had nearly been done to her (or what had been done, actually, since knowing someone was willing to do it was the same as it being done). Her endless goodbyes prevented her screaming at her parents, "Leaving me is not OK!"

That night in Amsterdam, she thought she saw Paolo in a club, and she pushed through the crowd, crestfallen when another man turned to her. Her avoidance of Italian restaurants softened; she had a disappointing Caprese salad and called him late that night to ask about his menu. He took the call.

She was noncommittal about her whereabouts and plans, though it was not that she knew and didn't want to tell him, it was that she didn't know her plans. She left Amsterdam, convincing herself she was following a series of art exhibits across the continent, but she was meandering. She went to Frankfurt (for the book fair, she told herself), to Zurich (for a week hiking in the mountains), then Milan (for a fashion show where a friend was debuting—she had to go!), and finally put her bags in a hotel in Florence, now fully aware of where she was headed.

She had been dreaming of Paolo every night since Amsterdam. The aroma of olive oil and garlic in Milan, and now especially in Florence, smelled like tenderness, aroused her with memories of the little room between dining and kitchen. No one else had made her feel this way. She'd had good lovers, good friends, people whose conversation was sparkling, others who shared her wayward journeying. But no one made her feel at home like Paolo, like the little village and the *trattoria* on the top of the hill. She shaved her legs, did her hair, got into a flowered dress she had purchased in Milan. Luca picked her up at the train station.

She hesitated at the entrance to the restaurant. *This may be the bravest thing I've ever done. Keep going, don't stop.* The bus boy ran for Paolo, and he walked toward her cautiously, wiping his hands on a cloth and removing his apron but not his cap. She stepped forward.

"I'm sorry. I'm so sorry."

"For what in particular?" he asked, as if daring her to recite the list.

"My mistakes so far, and the ones I know I'll make in the future."

He smiled slightly at the word "future." "There is no pre-forgiveness." He said it with mock sternness.

"I've never stayed, Paolo." She gestured back at the road that lead downhill and out of town. "This is the first time I've ever returned, and it scares me."

He took her in his arms and held her tightly.

About the Author

Jess Wells is the author of five novels and five books of short stories, and is the recipient of a San Francisco Arts Council Grant for Literature. Her work is included in more than three dozen anthologies and literary journals, has been reprinted in the UK and translated into Italian. Her previous historical fiction includes *A Slender Tether* (Fireship 2013), three compelling tales of self-discovery woven into a rich tapestry of 14th century France during Europe's Little Ice Age; *The Mandrake Broom* (Firebrand Books 2007), dramatizing the fight to save medical knowledge during the witch-burning times in Europe 1465-1540. Wells teaches writing at schools and conferences nation-wide.

For more information please visit Jess Wells:

Website:
http://www.jesswells.com

Facebook Page:
https://www.facebook.com/JessWellsAuthor

Book Club Guide

Fun ideas for book club meetings: There are few things more fun than a good book and a mug of hot chocolate so why not include chocolate treats in your meetings? Chocolate fondue recipes (with pound cake, strawberries, or banana slices for dipping) are easy to find on the Internet.

Chocolate fountains are inexpensive or can be rented from party stores. And after a discussion of the book, why not talk about your favorite chocolate bar during your childhood, and your favorite chocolate now? Are you a fan of milk chocolate, dark chocolate, or white chocolate? What is your favorite inclusion in chocolate, such as orange, caramel, nuts etc.? What is the strangest thing you've seen covered in chocolate or the oddest combination of flavors with chocolate?

Discussion Questions

1. Were you intrigued by the process of making chocolates in the story? Have you ever worked with chocolate?

2. The title of the book is *Straight Uphill*. How does this title relate to the topic of love?

3. Do any of the couples in the book seem like an unlikely pair?

4. There are many types of love described in the book. Discuss what they are. How many have you experienced?

5. The village in the story is a fictional representation of Coriglia in the Cinque Terre in Italy. What part of the village did you particularly like?

6. In the World War II section, do you think Caterina made the right decision to not use the poison?

7. Do you think there was any hope for Gretchen and Dario? Did you find Dario appealing?

8. What did you think of Paolo, the chef's son?

9. Is Kate's fear of intimacy understandable? Have you ever felt like running away rather than falling in love?

10. The author has a soft spot in her heart for Luca. Are his curmudgeonly nature and rugged good looks appealing? Can you see the draw between Luca and Adelina?

11. In the World War I section: what did you think of the life of Anya? Have you ever been faced with having to choose between love and freedom?

12. How did Capt. Zedoary change Delfina's life? What does Capt. Zedoary teach us about love?

13. In Anya's time, her request was for a life of freedom but in our time, it's sometimes more a question of self-fulfillment, empowerment, being free and being empowered to accomplish something. What do you think she would do if she lived in our time?

14. The author intended the World War I section to veer into a slightly more fantastical tone, especially at the end with the arrival of the appreciative recipients with their plaques. Did the arrival of the honorees brighten the book? Lift the story?

15. What mistakes did Gemma make with her daughters?

16. The author intended the section on chocolate in the 1400s to be fun. Did you like this section of the book? Do you feel the women were empowering themselves by taking over the chocolate preparation?

17. What did Bettina learn? What did she achieve?

18. Do you think that Gretchen made the right decision in the end?

19. How do you feel about the widows' park bench?

20. Two of the chocolatiers move in a very languid, almost hypnotic way when working with the chocolate. Have you ever felt that way cooking or doing any kind of hobby?

21. Can you describe each of the characters in terms of where they were in the beginning of the story and the end?

22. What are some of the most poignant moments in the book?

Enjoy other titles by Fireship Press

Courage Between Love and Death
Joseph Pillitteri

Elspeth has recently landed a nursing position. This is a big boon for her, but things are not going as expected. When the unthinkable happens, it is a turning point, not only for the medical industry and our country's security, but also for Elspeth personally. With her career and reputation on the line, will she have the courage to overcome the challenges she faces to clear her name and continue to be there for the ones she loves?

"...Joseph Pillitteri's writing is flawless and delightful. The tension builds up very fast and doesn't slow down until the satisfying conclusion... *Courage Between Love and Death* by Joseph Pillitteri is a historical novel that is well-researched and written to great satisfaction."

—Christian Sia, *Readers' Favorite*

Stone Circle
Kate Murdoch

When Antonius's father dies, he must work to support his family. He finds employment as a servant in the Palazzo Ducal, home of Conte Valperga. Sixteenth-century Pesaro is a society governed by status and Antonius has limited opportunities. When a competition is announced, Antonius seizes his chance. The winner will be apprenticed to the town seer. Antonius shares first place with his employer's son. The two men compete for their mentor's approval. As their knowledge of magic and alchemy grows, so does the rivalry and animosity between them. When the love of a beautiful woman is at stake, Antonius must find a way to follow his heart and navigate his future.

"In this debut historical fantasy, two young men become apprenticed to a seer during the Renaissance, igniting a rivalry for the man's daughter...Best of all, Murdoch delivers wisdom valuable to anyone trying to master a field: 'Those who are consumed by negative thoughts about others cannot possibly reach the level of purity required.' Despite a clever, definitive ending, readers may clamor for a sequel. Italy sparkles in this layered 16th-century romance." **—*Kirkus Reviews***

Cortero

An Imprint of Fireship Press

Interesting • Informative • Authoritative

All Cortero books are available through
leading bookstores and wholesalers worldwide.